Additional Praise for *The Quickening*

"*The Quickening* is a rare jewel of a novel: an elegantly structured page-turner driven as much by its exquisite lyricism as by the gripping story at its core. It wondrously weaves a riveting half century of American Midwestern history through the sensual, intimate, often strange details that make up a life. Michelle Hoover is a stunning writer, and this is a fierce and beautiful book." —MAUD CASEY, author of *Genealogy*

"*The Quickening*, through its carefully wrought, precise prose, builds with a heartrending power that lingers long after the final page. Michelle Hoover is a writer to watch." —DON LEE, author of *Wrack and Ruin*

"From the opening pages of this beautiful novel, I found myself immersed in the lives of these two farm women between the wars and their struggles with their families, themselves, the land, and each other. *The Quickening* is such a fully realized, sensually vivid, psychologically intelligent novel that it's hard to believe it is a debut, but it is, and a sparkling one." —MARGOT LIVESEY, author of *The House on Fortune Street*

"Just as the women and men in this strikingly assured debut novel wrest life out of the land they work, Michelle Hoover wrests from her characters' hearts, and from this heart-touching story, understandings rich in complexity and compassion. She paints the intricacies of their interiors as skillfully as she does the details of the world that surrounds them. What a gift she has given us in this wise book that lets us so vividly experience both." —JOSH WEIL, author of *The New Valley*

The Quickening

A NOVEL

MICHELLE HOOVER

OTHER PRESS • NEW YORK

Copyright © 2010 Michelle Hoover

Parts of this novel appeared, in an earlier form, in *The Massachusetts Review, Prairie Schooner, Confrontation,* and *Best New American Voices 2004.*

Production Editor: *Yvonne E. Cárdenas*
Book design: *Simon M. Sullivan*
This book was set in 11.75 pt Bell by Alpha Design & Composition of Pittsfield, NH.

10 9 8 7 6 5 4 3

Library of Congress Cataloging-in-Publication Data

Hoover, Michelle.
The quickening / Michelle Hoover.
p. cm.
ISBN 978-1-59051-346-0 (pbk. original with flaps) — ISBN 978-1-59051-360-6 (e-book) 1. Neighbors—Fiction. 2. Farm life--Fiction. 3. Domestic fiction. I. Title.
PS3608.O6253Q53 2010
813'.6—dc22
2010005199

PUBLISHER'S NOTE:
This is a work of fiction. Names, characters, places, and incidents either are the product of the author's imagination or are used fictitiously, and any resemblance to actual persons, living or dead, events, or locales is entirely coincidental.

For my mother, Lorene,
her mother, Angelie,
and her mother, Melva

Contents

Enidina

(*Summer 1913–Spring 1914*)

My boy, you might think an old woman hasn't much to say about the living, but your grandmother knows when a person does right by her and when they don't. In this bed, I have little else to do but scratch my life down with this pencil. And I have little left to me but the thought of you my grandchild who I've known only in the warmth of your mother's belly under my hand. Even if you never come home, you should understand the way our life once was, your grandfather, your mother, and I, and all the little things that make its loss so very terrible in my mind. The Morrow family, they were a worry to ours from day one. And once you know what they took from us, you might just understand the kind of people you come from.

It wasn't until late in the summer of 1913 that your grandfather and I began to work this farm from the acres of weeds and grasses it was to a fine place. A place where we could earn a living. That's what a beginning is. My father and his father and his father before that had lived within the same ten square miles of land. Even after I married, I didn't move farther from home than a day's wagon ride. I'd seen no other landscape as a child. Had never dreamt of it. A farm is where I was born. Where I would always live. I'd known it from the day my mother walked me through the fields and rubbed her fingers in the dirt, putting her thumb to my mouth so I could taste the dust and seed we lived on. She said this was home. When I asked her if there was anything else, she shook her head. "Nowhere you need pay any mind to," she said. "Not for the likes of us."

It was only a month after I'd lost my father that Frank and I first came to this place. We married on a Sunday, as Frank thought right, the chapel holding only our families and a few friends. There we stood, both in our thirties, Frank the older by eight years and graying at the temples. He wore a borrowed suit that showed his ankles and wrists, I in a dove-colored dress, my red hair combed smooth to lessen my height. Afterward we ate cake and berries and they tasted too sweet. We opened our gifts. My mother swept a spot of frosting from my chin and drew out my arms to look at the fit of my dress. I'd always been a big woman, suited more for the farm than for marrying, an old bride as I was back then. My cousins had to squint to find the ring on my hand.

Only late did we return to what Frank had made our home. This same house, with borrowed furniture in the rooms. The house smelled of earth and smoke. Frank had polished the wood and swept the floors, leaving the broom to rest on the front porch. He'd spent most of his years working to buy the house and land, much of it still in sorry condition. Though he didn't speak of it, his family were croppers. He'd seldom had a thing of his own. Now the both of us had a fair bit, and after the loss of my father, I was as determined as Frank to keep it. When I hurried in, Frank took that broom under his arm and strummed me a song, a sorry frown on his face when he pretended the broom had snapped a string. I grinned, dropping a penny at his feet. This was my husband, a string of a man himself with a good bit of humor in him. He was fair-skinned with black hair and long limbs, his eyes fainter than any blue I'd ever seen. If anything, I knew him to be kind and hardworking, and that was enough. Behind a curtain of chintz was the bed he'd made. The sheets were white and damp with the weather, and in the night they proved little warmth. Outside, the animals in the barn were still. I could smell them through the window. But inside, this was what marriage was.

I'd left those ten square miles and moved to the next county over, a place that looked and smelled the same as my father's land. The difference was my part in this place. I was a wife, and not until that night did I know what the word meant.

It was still dark the next morning when I carried water back from the well, wearing the whitest skirts I owned. I filled a large basin in the smokehouse, dunked the bed sheets in. The water in the basin reddened. The stain on the sheets loosened and spread. It was the same that had stained me in the early morning and sent Frank hurrying away to milk. My mother had told me if a husband was easy, if he was a good man, the first night wouldn't be trouble. "Maybe it will be better," she'd said. But she hadn't said a word about this. In the smokehouse, my hands puckered from the long time I scrubbed. The sheets turned a muddy pink, my chest and arms wet. The light of my kerosene lamp fell against the skin of hogs hung to smoke, a gift to us, their torsos stripped and twisting slow on the hooks caught in their spines.

Outside I kicked the basin over, let the bloody water sink into the dirt. There were fewer trees around the house then. They did not make much noise in the wind. Gnats and midges circled my feet, a knocking in my chest. A good man, I thought. But Frank was nearly a stranger to me, as I was to him. Beyond that stain, a mist crept over the fields. The land seemed barren in the early morning, not another living creature. In only two months was the harvest and we would be planting late. We wouldn't have much to keep us through winter. The night before had given me a full-up feeling, a kind of lightness and pain. But with the smell of meat from the smokehouse and the dark-wetted dirt, that feeling turned into misgiving. When finally I'd gathered myself, I pinned those sheets to the line where they whipped together and I left them for the sun.

In the kitchen I fixed a pot of oats and filled a pan with milk, the milk trembling around my spoon as I stirred. At the door of my parents' house, my mother had waited only days before with a jar of jam under her arm, raising her chin to see us go off. With my father gone, she rented out the land and kept the house to herself, an arrangement that would agree with her for many years more. She was a small woman, my mother. Her skirts she hemmed nearly twice as high as my own and still they grew ragged from the ground. But she had a steadiness to her and a strength that made her larger in that doorway than most men. My mother wouldn't speak of her worries about me. She wasn't the kind. Still, that jar of rhubarb jam seemed as red as her cheeks just then, and the sky, she said, it didn't look right. When I took it from her, the jar was warm, but as I held it close to me in the wagon, it cooled. I had my bedclothes and pillows with me. I had a trunk full of notions. But with that jam, I knew I could carry my mother for only a short while. Now opening the jar again, my eyes teared as I brushed my thumb through. The jam tasted grainy and thick. When I let it hang on the tip of my thumb and tasted it again, it soothed the cracks of my skin and filled my mouth with sweetness.

Outside, the sheets clapped together. If I squinted right, I could imagine a child playing between them. In the wind, the sheets caught the child up and lifted him giggling from the dirt. If I could have squinted well enough, I'd have brought that child straight into this house. I'd have heard him stepping in, boots on his feet. With Frank's black hair and blue eyes I imagined him, and the heavy hands that were his mother's, suited more to a boy than any young woman. Children are a way of keeping things, or so I once believed. They plant you to this earth, give you roots to stay a while. Now in the kitchen, I wondered just how long it would be until I had one of my own. With that boy stamping his feet on our floor, I'd have asked if he wanted some jam. If he opened his mouth, I would have held my finger out.

The wind rose. Like a clock the sheets ticked against their line, counting the time I would sit and wait for Frank to return.

In the fall we spent mornings in the barn. Back then we had a dozen cows, sixteen hogs, four hens, and two horses.

We had a few tons of hay and fifty bushels of corn. When the light came, we worked the fields and saved what we'd planted from rot, late in the season as our planting was. Our farm was a hundred and eighty acres, straight and fine as you could want with hardly a tree or stone to break it, as most of it was bottomland. The sky here was low and wide. A place you could spy the weather from a good ways off. Our house sat like a small wooden marker in the countryside. Stooped and curiously held together, hidden by the shade of trees. The porches lay level to the dust and fields. Acres of farmland stretched in every direction, gray-green and buzzing. The gravel road that cuts across our yard, it did so even then. Most of it was mud and stones and suited more for horses than the trucks that rumble past now. The sharp, sweet stink of mud and pigs rode the wind, our barn alone against the distance. Splitting the chores between us, Frank and I often worked without sight of the other until evening. That's where I was then, out weeding the rows by hand with the shoots I pulled my only company. The Morrows were our only neighbors for miles.

"Hard work," a voice called out. I turned my head. A woman stood stalk-straight in my field. She was nearly my own age but pale-skinned. The shawl over her shoulders was the color of gold. Our house lay at her back, a path between her and it, as if she'd just walked from the place herself. A spirit, I thought, drifting as she seemed and too delicate for such country. The way she twitched reminded me of a bird.

"Wouldn't be work if it wasn't," I answered.

"But it's awful hard, isn't it? And hot as a buzzard. I don't think I've ever seen dust like this. Like it'll never wash off."

That's the way she went, you see, talking as if she was thirsty, but not for anything I felt good enough to offer. She talked as if she had never talked to another person in her life. "Those potatoes won't be good for much," she went on. "Not this late, I mean. Not unless you boil them. Of course, if you don't plant the right kind, boiling will turn them to mush. Maybe it's best you throw them away."

I studied her then. She was speaking rubbish, throwing good food away. On closer look, with that shawl over her like a garland and so early in the daytime, I guessed she might do such a thing. "I don't suppose that'd be right," I said. My hands were raw from pulling weeds. Three hours at the work and the soil covered me head to toe. "Enidina," I offered at last, sitting up on my knees. "Though my husband calls me Eddie. Only him." I wiped my hand from the sweat and dirt and held it out.

"Mary Morrow," she said with a grimace. My hand nearly swallowed her own. "We're neighbors," she said. "Over there, less than half a mile. Ours is an even longer trip to town." With a lift of her chin, she showed me her house in the distance, a hard brick face against the fields. What with that look of hers, I knew we were farther from each other than that run of dirt road between us.

You may think me unfriendly, but I have trouble remembering Mary without uneasiness. Even then, I was wary of strangers, and I believed women were especially difficult. I had no sisters to speak of. Had only my mother now and three brothers, gone off to have families of their own. Though I'd tried for friendship, their wives never much cared for the youngest sister who worked with the men in the barn. But women had never liked the look of me. Saw something fierce in my size and roughness. Mary seemed no different. That grimace of hers, it was just the start.

"The big place," she said. She turned to look at our own and tugged that shawl close to her chest. Next to hers, our house seemed a low stack of wood, but an honest one. The kind people could grow into. The afternoon had hushed and the soil was sticky in my palms. As I stood, I wondered just what she wanted with us. "Now, look at you," she said. "Just look." Her eyes narrowed and a smile came to her lips. "We have two boys ourselves and I knew with both of them. In only weeks, I knew it." She reached out to touch my dress. "You're carrying."

I stepped away from her and looked down at my stomach and feet. I was black with dirt and had wiped my hands on my middle so many times that I'd stained my dress with fingerprints. "Isn't that a wonder," I said. I didn't know until then, you see. I'd felt something coming. Like a rainstorm I'd felt it, but burrowing inside me. I'd been sick for so many months, sick too after my father's death. I hadn't bothered to pay attention to the weight I'd taken on in our bed or any child it might promise. Mary said her piece and I believed it then, reddening at the thought that this woman had known before me. In her fancy shawl and curious ways, she'd taken the surprise that was mine alone.

I bent to my work to answer her, hoping to end the visit as fast as it'd begun. "It's not so terrible to know before your time," she said. But I would have none of it. Her voice was sharp and all too sure of itself. She looked mighty pleased. I kept my back to her, and her feet scratched at the ground like one of our chickens. Finally she walked away.

A sour taste rose at the back of my throat as I watched her go, but the sourness was different now. It had its reasons. "Carrying," she'd said. With my brothers' wives, I'd stayed outside in the parlor with the men. In the barn, birthing was a dark, bloody business. The last I'd seen left the cow panting on her knees. We buried her afterward in the snow. Mary stumbled as she went, that gold glinting in her shawl, and I felt the emptiness of this place. The dirt in the fields stirred with insects and wind. The sun was an awful brightness. This woman had carried two children herself. Despite her looks, she'd done that. Against all I'd heard of the ways of strangers, I called after her to welcome her again, and she offered a wave back. She has never left us quite alone since.

We had the rest of the fall to ourselves before Mary came with her family, the first real visitors to our place. Walking into the corner of my kitchen, she studied the weight of my chest and stomach. Her eyes passed over our countertops like a finger feeling for dust. We had but four plates and these my mother had spared us. Surprised by their arrival at dinnertime, Frank and I had to share a plate between us, as did Mary and her youngest. I opened a jar of meat and boiled some noodles, warmed a sugar dressing for our lettuce. The bread I'd baked during the week I hoped might fill the meal, a cup of broth to soften the crust. I laid out the meat and noodles in my roasting pan, as I had no other dishes, and I kept our only apples for dessert. When Frank set the last plate in front of Mary's husband, Jack looked at Frank's hand and wondered at it. Jack's own was scarred and wide and never much for serving, or so I guessed. Taking hold of the plate himself, Jack righted it at a proper distance for his fork and knife, but Frank didn't seem to mind. Quiet as he was before a meal, Frank took his seat, his eyes closed and hands on the table. Mary did the same. In the silence, Mary's youngest knocked over his water glass.

"Are you done?" Mary asked, studying the boy.

Her youngest turned quiet. Mary stood and gave him a cool pinch on the cheek. When she went to clear the mess, the napkin in her hand came away darkly stained. "Well," she said, "this table needs a wash."

My fork struck our plate.

"Don't you worry," Frank let out. His eyes were open now and bright. With a glance, I knew he was talking to me and the boy both. "I must do that every day myself," Frank said. "In fact, I did it just this morning, with a bowl of oatmeal. What do you think of that?" Frank took the boy's chin between finger and thumb. The boy buckled and grinned. He wasn't much more than two, and shied from his mother's arm as she scrubbed.

"Interrupting your mother's prayers . . . ," Mary said. "And this man, he was praying too." The cuffs of Mary's blouse looked neat against her wrists, her nails trimmed.

The way she'd sat so stiffly at our table, I knew she kept herself separate from our place. Her boys were pale too, raised soft by their mother and flushed in the heat of the kitchen. But in a few years they were to be farmer's sons.

"That's all right, Mary," Frank said. "It's plenty clean now."

"But a man when he's praying," Mary went on, "he needs quiet. A woman needs it too. When they're expecting a child, they need all the help they can. Isn't that right, Jack?"

"Mary," Jack said, but Mary took hold of his arm and he left off. His fingers had tightened around his knife, but her hand seemed to settle him. A large man, Jack looked uneasy in our kitchen, his arms straining his sleeves. His face was rough and tan and darkened easily, his eyes sharp and strangely colored in the deep folds of a squint. He chewed at his meat. A fire in his silence, he stared out the window as if to count the worthy rows of our field.

"A baptism," Mary started again. "That's what your child needs. Mother and child both." She went on as if offering a sermon, talking with her hands over our cooling plates. I'd heard about these baptisms. The music and prayers, a day's walk out to a large enough lake to have it done. They dressed to be drowned, these followers. A worn, white shirt, a dress that could be ruined, a robe. Cheap fabrics believed good enough to keep a person afloat. No one wore shoes except the minister. No one could spare the expense. The water was cold stepping in, a cause for sickness. The women's skirts floated to the surface. The men left their hats ashore. There were prayers, a lowering of faces, and too much sun. As Mary talked, I wondered just what she thought such a soaking would do for us. "Before you're too far along," she said.

"I'm not so sure about that," I let out.

Frank turned to me then. For a man with such an easy tongue, he had a slow way of asking for things. Quiet in his meanings. I was used to this with my brothers, that silence in a man when his sense of right and wrong slips. He has no speech to tackle it. Frank's face took on a look of desperateness. As if he knew what I was thinking, he took hold of my hand.

"That's right, Frank," Mary said. "It'll be your child too." But she said it looking at me.

When finally I agreed to it, I agreed because Frank had asked it of me. If we were having a child, it would be mine and Frank's both. But I didn't really think there was a place with so much water. And I didn't think there would be so many interested in seeing it done.

We walked out miles past our house, more than a dozen of us in a ragged line. It was dark starting and we carried lanterns. No one spoke, though the rocks under our feet made sound enough. By the time we reached the end of the road, the morning sun gave some light, all of us filthy with dust. Most of the others were women. And most of these had such a glazed look in their eyes, I feared I would soon look the same. The road narrowed into a stand of trees. As the trees cleared, the sun broke onto a wide stretch of water. I stopped and pulled at Frank's hand. Children crowded the shore in dozens, their mothers gripping their shoulders. These were the curious. Not members of the church. They'd ridden from town in carriages and the men stayed back to tend to the horses. Mary stood alone out front, her hands clasped beneath her chin. Her dress was pale and long, like a robe itself, and a line of church members waited at her back. "All right," Frank said and swallowed. "Just a few folks." He smiled at me and tugged my hand. When at last I waded into the lake, Frank stepped in himself up to his knees. Soon there I was, waist deep in the water and shivering at the head of the line, for I was the first to be baptized.

The minister wore a suit and button-front shirt all in white, as I'd never seen on a man before. Borden was his name. That summer, he and his father had only just raised their church when the older man suffered a stroke, or so I'd been told. His son was left for the ministering, new though he was in the area and alone. With his black hair and eyes, his blue-white skin, Borden was tall and easy to look at if you cared to for long. He hung his coat on the branch of a tree and stepped into the lake, a hitch in his stride as he went. "Are we ready?" he said. I looked for Frank by the shore. He waved. I nodded to Borden then and he touched my forehead, lowering me back. Borden's hands were clean and white. Not a hardworking man. Religious. He would never understand what it meant to pray to a field. To feed and watch over the animals that ruled the fat of our stomachs. We looked in hope to the ground and the roots growing there more often than we looked for grace from the sky. He dipped us under and stumbled when we sank too fast.

Red-faced as he tried to lift us up again, he was afraid. You could see it. The one coming out of the water, like a newborn, might forget how to breathe.

I was a heavy woman then as I am still and heavier while I was carrying. Borden lost hold of me and I felt a rush of water. Beneath the surface, I imagined that boy from the laundry line again, swimming up to me from the bottom. His arms and chest were white and thin, his cheeks swollen from holding his breath. He swept a tangle of weeds from his eyes and took hold of my arms. With his face close to mine, I believed I'd known him my whole life. I'd already given birth to him. Already raised him in my house. When finally I felt the air again, I took it in. There came a flash of color, a confusion of hands. I stood in the sun and blinked. The boy was gone. "You are blessed," Borden called. The church members echoed, "You are blessed."

I caught hold of myself, my dress clinging to me. The people on the shore watched and waited, their horses pawing the dirt. Mary's blessing rose above the rest like a hiss. She gazed at Borden where he clung to my hand and seemed about to rush into the lake between us. I shivered where I stood, my dress soaked clear through. My belly was swollen and plain to see. I must have looked close to naked underneath. Frank rushed into the water and wrapped his jacket around my waist, but it was too late. Everyone had seen, and they would expect a child from me.

Some mornings after, I awoke in a sweat and felt for Frank where he slept. His face burned against his pillow, his forehead hot, cheeks flushed. I would not wake him to his fever but sat back in our bed, hoping the fever would lift. Rain drove through the fields. The morning was dark and the darkness had let me sleep late. Next to me, Frank's chest rose and fell, and I rested my hand on my stomach. If I waited long enough, I believed I might feel the child inside me stirring.

My boy, you may not understand how awful this waiting was. In those years, you never could be sure of a child, no matter how soon in coming. And you never took for granted what a birth might cost the mother herself. The skin of my belly jumped. I pressed my hand against it again and whispered Frank's name. Outside, the storm rattled the eaves, but Frank slept on. I felt his forehead. When at last he woke, the strain of his voice came from a dimmer place, and his eyes watered against the light of the lamps.

Mary had become a regular visitor on Saturdays, but that morning she arrived late. "It's bad today, Eddie," she said. "Your yard's breaking up." I could barely hear her, so loud was the rain outside. Cold and dripping on our front porch, Mary and her good looks seemed to slide away, strange to me. I leaned against the wall.

"What's wrong?" she said.

"Frank needs a doctor."

"But we can't go anywhere in this weather," she said. "It wasn't bad when I set out, but now . . ." Mary left off, helping herself from her wet coat. Her legs and shoes were thick with earth, as if she'd crawled her way along the road. Outside, the rain had grown heavy, carrying the mud away with it. I knew at once no buggy could cross that ground. No horse could even draw it, not with the weight of a man. The baby crouched against my stomach, and I placed my hands beneath it, feeling it could fall.

"Has he been fed?" Mary asked.

"Some broth to work against his fever. I think it's all he should have."

"A man must eat, Eddie."

"You're not supposed to make it difficult for his system."

"Starving's not hard? I'll give him some meat."

Frank called my name then. I let her go and sat to take his hand. Frank was the one I worried about. His fingers were white in mine, his face thin. After a while he opened his light-colored eyes. The wind outside swept the house, and our roof shifted beneath it. When at last Mary reappeared from our kitchen, she held a cold leg of chicken on a fork and snapped her fingers at me.

"I don't want him to have any of that," I said at once.

"What now? After all my trouble?"

"That's trouble of your own choosing."

Frank stirred and I thought of my father when he grew ill, laid out in our home where we'd tried to tend to him. For weeks he shivered under every blanket we owned, coughed up the tonics we gave him and refused more. Nothing we did seemed enough.

"Look at him," Mary said. "My cousin was sick like this. You should have seen his wife's face when the doctor claimed she'd tried to kill him. For days she hadn't fed him anything more than broth."

I didn't answer. I could imagine the look on that wife's face as clearly as my own. I didn't know about doctoring. And I didn't know what would be worse for a man, a bite of chicken or two women in a quarrel over his bed. My father had refused doctors himself, leaving us at his bedside with our hands in our laps. Before I could even raise my head, Mary had dropped a piece of chicken into Frank's open mouth. "There," she said. "The meat will give you strength."

There wasn't much use in doubting her now. Frank slept after he ate, and Mary and I sat in our corners, impatient in the silence between us as we watched over my husband. It was a while he slept. We spoke about the rain, about the animals and our chores, our voices low as if in some holy place. "Never seen a storm like this," Mary said. "Why, I almost didn't come. Where would you have been then?"

"I suppose I'd be in the same place," I answered. "Though Frank would be without his chicken. That would be the difference."

Mary made a kind of hiccup at that, but I knelt beside Frank and pretended not to hear. Even in his sleep, Frank seemed calm and distant.

"Mary," I said. "He won't wake."

"He's sleeping."

"He's not."

"But he's breathing." She went to slap his cheek.

"You've done enough," I said, catching her hand, and she winced. I wrapped my shawl over my head, found my boots and coat, and layered on what else I could before turning for the door.

"Where are you going?"

"For the doctor."

"You can't carry a baby through this."

I looked at her. Her hair had stuck to her forehead in drying and her dress was stained with mud and grass. "You could come with me," I said.

"But somebody's got to stay here. Somebody should."

"And that would be you?"

Mary backed away from me then, rubbing her arms. I shook my head at such a woman, keeping to her place in the warm, dry room she'd always hated. It had been building in us, this tugging at each other, sitting so still as we waited beneath the rain for Frank to wake. As I opened the door, the rain wet my hands and I stepped into the storm.

It would be six miles to town. I pushed through the mud and tried to keep myself steady, listening to the wind as it whipped about and blew the shawl from around my head. With the shawl gone, I felt full out in the storm. The rain burned my cheeks. It stung through the gaps of my coat. With my hands raw and numb, I held on to the fence posts where they lined the road and I crouched beneath the weather, one arm over my face and the other beneath my stomach for warmth. It was luck that kept me to that road when I was pushed from it by the wind. When gusts turned me in circles and ran me into the fields. I was bleary with mud, thick with the stuff where I wiped my face, sweeping my hair back so I could see. When finally I found the doctor's door, I could only lean against it and rattle the knob, hoping the doctor would hear.

I'd spent the rest of the daylight and more in that struggle to town, but it took only an hour to reach home again. As I stepped in, the noises in my head confused many things: the length of our return, the doctor and I, my journey through the storm and back. When finally I'd reached him, the doctor was tired and angry. The tail of his coat whipped behind him as he stood in the rain, cranking his car until the engine turned. I'd never before ridden in a car myself. When the mud caught the wheels, we left it behind and walked the last mile. In that mile we saw the worst of the storm, the way it tricked us. It drove us to our knees in the mud before the wind and rain delivered us into the house.

In the time since I'd left, the house had again grown quiet. Mary sat with her eyes on the door, her hands folded in a blanket as if she'd wrung the blanket in waiting. I dropped into our bed next to Frank and heard Mary speak at last to the doctor, explaining my husband's fever and what we'd done. The doctor scolded me for the chicken. Mary hovered near, her hands cupped over her mouth and whispering to herself. Often in the years to come, I would see her when she thought I wasn't looking, whispering just like that. A whole book of whispering whenever her luck ran dry, as if God Himself listened at her feet. I tried to keep my eyes open and heard my husband stir against his pillow, the sharp words of the doctor, and Mary's nervous tongue. As

I fell asleep, it was this that filled my head, empty of Mary's speeches now, her watery gods, her assurances. She agreed with the doctor's opinions against me as if she'd entirely forgotten her part. I was too beaten with rain to say anything in my defense.

The rest was sleep for a while. The doctor moved about us, it seemed, for weeks. Frank and I traded our sicknesses, and I stayed in bed after Frank grew well. My dreams were rain and wind, spinning me where I slept. The baby was born still.

II

Mary
(*Fall 1909–Fall 1913*)

This could not be the place my new husband had brought me, it could not be where Jack meant us to live. This man who enclosed my hand in his and sent a shiver straight to my veins, he could never sink so low as to think this house could be our home.

Still there he was, full of his green-eyed mischief. Something warm curled inside my chest. He bounded through the entrance, bent to his knee, and when he opened his arms I let myself cross that threshold and fall in—because that was the way it was back then, Jack with his wide, sturdy hands, his stubbornness, his strength, a burning in him that made me soft, magnificent, believing there was only talk and waiting in this world unless I was with him.

So I worked at this house to make it my own—a gaping ship of a place, with two floors and more space than we could ever hope to fill. The rooms above me whined in the silence and heat. I spent mornings on my knees, scraping at the filth that blackened the floors, and learned in all my labor about the family that squandered their luck here at the turn of the century, having overbuilt, overplanted, and abandoned the house after seven years—I swore the same would never happen to us. After I scrubbed the windows and stripped the curtains, I left my rags and rubbish in a pile outside for Jack to burn. He carried in buckets of water before he set off for the barn, tossed the gray runoff when he returned home. Sweeping off his hat, he wondered at the rooms I had made, bright and smelling of soap, and at the state of my dress, my hunger for something clean. I kept at this house with a heavy hand the first years we stayed, shook the outdoors from the rugs and bolted the windows. When my sons were born, when they grew to stand and watch their father cutting like a knife through the fields, I kept them in too—because if anything, I wanted to hold them in that lifted-up place I believed was promised us, in that place where we were better than all the rest and more deserving, and with my sons it would not just be a far-off belief or a kind of pretending. It would be.

But there is only so much a person can do beyond wishing. In my mother's house, I was taught to walk in heels and carry cups of tea, though guests were rare back then. I sat alone in our parlor with my legs crossed, hands in my lap, and spoke only when spoken to. Beyond our windows, neighbors passed with their heads turned or crossed to the far side of the street. They no longer came to our door for my father's woodwork, let alone for company. On a long, flat board, I learned to play my scales on keys my father had etched with his knife into the wood—because even if we did not have a piano, my mother was determined that her daughter with her long fingers would be able to play in any house in town that did.

"The accident," my parents called it, though my father said little if he could. It had happened just after I turned twelve, remaining with me like a dull haze through my teenage years. All I knew was how strange I felt one morning, sick to my stomach with an aching in my legs and just under my chin. This was not the way it had been, my parents seemed to be saying, the quietness of our house and our neighbors who kept their watch over us. After the accident, everything had changed and I was somehow the reason.

"Practice every day," my mother instructed. When I ran my fingers over the board my father had given me, she hummed the tune, stumbling whenever she believed I had struck the wrong key. What little my mother remembered from her childhood lessons, she remembered fiercely—to keep time, she beat a wooden ruler against my arm until the skin burned.

"It will never be enough, will it?" she said, stopping the thump of that stick. I lifted my fingers from practicing while my mother gazed at the wall over my head. The ruler cut into her fist and a scar showed jagged along her knuckles—the scar invisible except when she grew nervous and her hands blushed. A boy with a temper had been jealous with her, she had told me, long before she met my father. I had to be careful of such boys, she said. Now with her standing so still, I thought I might reach out to touch her—there where that long, hot slice broke her skin—and its warmth would share itself with me and be mine for a while. When I was younger, before the accident, it had been different—my mother's palm warm against the middle of my back whenever we were close enough to touch. Now she shook her head and I dropped my hands to the wooden keys. "No, it will," she said. "It will be if we want it. We can have everything again as long as we are good and persevering. Mary, you just have to believe what I tell you. Never let anyone get in your way."

We were no longer considered a fine family, but in her every hour, my mother relied a great deal on seeming.

"Someday you'll know better," my father told me. He was a quiet man, already stooped, spending his waking hours in the shed where he worked. I thought then my father's words were offering me a better kind of living, but later I knew he had meant how gray those days would seem, the polite and constant practicing, when what I wanted was something glowing and passionate and strange.

When first I met Jack, it was his voice that shook me, echoing out of a storefront where he argued with the owner inside—I stopped at once, wondering what kind of man could have a voice like that, as large as daylight. He cursed and a case in the store broke, knuckles into glass. He rushed out the door with the owner yelling and I saw him then, turning one way and the next, not knowing what to do with himself. "I'll pay for it all right," he yelled back. He leaned against the porch rail an arm's reach from me and stared at the ground. I scratched my foot against the dirt until he looked up, his green eyes rising over my face without expression. When his mouth opened without a word, I felt swallowed up whole.

Later I would learn that Jack was the youngest in a family of men, that his mother had died a year after he was born. They were only a father and five brothers, the father lost to work and drink and the sons all born into a four-room farmhouse far in the East where they sweated for women in their bunks. His brothers had raised him with their fists and jokes, my husband nodding without a word whenever I asked to know more. But I could imagine the way that house had been, the heat of all those boys as they worked the farm and cooked their meals, a charred crust of fat and bloody meat in the saucepan. It was a place of temper and few words, the taste of smoke and salt—boys playing mother to each other, their feet muddy in the kitchen. Because that was the kind of place where Jack must have been born, the hard muscle of a man that he was and still so much a boy.

Jack stood against the rail, his overalls wind-whipped and dull, breaking at the seams. The straps hung loose at his thighs and his thighs were thick and muscled under the denim. The skin of his knuckles had broken into bloody streaks and he bound his hand in his shirt.

"You'll never get your price like that," I said.

For a moment he only stared. I took a step back, the store's brick front hard against my spine.

"I know it," he swore, sweeping off his cap and twisting it between his fingers. "I was never much the bartering kind." He shrugged with a smile and dropped his head. It was then that what had seemed devilish in Jack fell away, as if he were a child—his face streaked by the sun, his eyes green and squinting, and the crown of his hair standing on end.

What a wonder, I thought, the way such a man could hold both at once, all that rage and innocence, and I had been the one to bring that innocence out.

I was twenty-two years old the day we met, Jack over thirty—we would marry later that year at my mother's house with only my parents to witness the event. He was born a wanderer, my Jack— he had no family or friends of his own nearby to invite. Ever since he was young, he had worked to get as far as possible from that four-room farmhouse, and by the time I met him, he had traveled a great deal, from the dark, narrow countryside of the East, little more than a nickel in his pocket. But that husband of mine had cunning. He could smell the stench of a family's foolishness from a distance, so our farm he got for a dime, troubled as the place had been and abandoned for over a year. I was the one who had stopped him in his traveling, or so he said, the one who had made him want to think about building a home. Carrying me off as he did more than a week's ride from my parents, Jack found a ground he could root his fevers in, and I knew with those green eyes of his that I had traveled and stopped as well—all before I got the chance to do otherwise.

For the first four years, our house never did lose that ache to fall back into the wreck it had been. I kept at my work to clean it, and my husband returned only at dusk, bringing in the weather on his boots and the barn stink—a wildness, despite all that could be steady in him and warm. Upstairs

my sons grew and fidgeted in their beds, drooling on the
sheets with wide, hungry mouths—always wanting. Yet if
I should want to hold them, they wearied and twisted their
limbs like animals out of my grip.

I had a gold-threaded shawl of silk my mother had given
me for our wedding, and late in the afternoons I took to
sitting when I could in an empty room on the second floor
and wrapped the shawl around me. The windows looked
out over the fields, the trees bent and withered against the
dust. There was the grayness again—earth, brush, and
wind—not even birds rested for long on that ground. If I
said Jack's name aloud in that room, it would sound as hard
as metal, and if I opened the windows, the sound would
travel over the fields without so much as a tree or hill large
enough to break it, without anyone to hear save for the animals wrenching the grass with their teeth. When it circled
back again, I imagined it running against this house with
its hard brick front. I imagined it finding me again in this
room, echoing where I sat for hours with that shawl knotted around my neck.

It was only when I turned to face the windows to the
west that I saw a difference—a small house that stood on
the horizon like a stone. I watched it for a whole year until
one day smoke came rushing from the chimney.

"You're hiding," my husband whispered. He stood in the
doorway, gripping the frame. I turned back to my window
and the smoke. There it is at last, I wanted to say, a sign of
the living. My husband rested his hands on my shoulders
and I realized how much I was in need of company, something feminine and soft.

"See that?" I tapped my finger on the windowpane. Inside the house, I imagined a woman sat at her own window after the afternoon chores, looking out and seeing us, a large place less than a mile out. She was a young wife herself, and she tucked her hands into her lap to keep warm in the winters or turned a fan in front of her face against the heat. Her children were already in their beds, that slow time of day when a woman has a chance to think—and what she thought was this: there must be more in this place if a person goes far enough. Jack crouched to look out, his hands weighing into my shoulders, all that was hungry in me still rising to his presence. Upstairs, my sons woke from their nap and bounded down the steps, their voices pitched, calling for supper. I saw myself knocking on the woman's door, the hearth inside and a meal with tomatoes and fresh cream, a clean tablecloth. In the mornings, we would press bread together and work our gardens, and in the afternoons I would help the woman bleach her linens and can fruit and meats. Girls she would have, two of them, and they would make my own boys quiet and thoughtful, good to their mother. Jack cleared his throat and kissed me quickly on the cheek—but when I looked in the glass, his face was silent and dark. Ever since our first night in the house, Jack had studied me the way a mother studies a child with its hands behind its back. Sometimes even children are innocent, I wanted to say, but Jack never would let me forget—the sheets appeared clean and white that first morning when we woke, though we had become a husband and wife in every sense.

"The old Bowers place," he said at last. "They should have a hard time of it." He clapped me on the shoulder and walked out. I could still smell the work on him, felt it sink into my skin with all its sweat and noise and dirt. My fingers moved lightly over the pane, my hands feeling for the notes. Girls, I thought, and the woman sang while I played her piano, her hair tied back with pins. My husband had left me alone in my room, but I could sense him still watching for me from the hall. My sons were in the kitchen, their hands I imagined too close to the stove, red and blistering, waiting for me to snatch them back. The house itself ached for my attention—even in my sleep I heard it suffer in the wind. When I looked out the window again, I caught my breath—the afternoon had darkened, my reflection suddenly bone-thin, and I feared everything in me that had been bright and young could die in this place before I ever turned thirty.

It took weeks until I finally set out on foot, walking toward the house I had seen because the horizon held little else. I carried nothing with me, wore only a housedress and easy shoes, wrapping my mother's shawl around my shoulders in case of wind. How far I would go I left to hunger, weariness, or chance—but surely there was a place where the sun did not shine so brightly, where I could stand against the trunk of a tree and listen to the creak of its limbs, not have to worry about the weather or the state of the soil beneath my feet. The back of my neck grew wet from walking, the fields liquid under the sun. Insects clung to the stalks with a humming that covered my skin with dust. I still had that neighbor woman at her window well in mind, and if she could lead a horse, I thought, we might go as a pair to the market in town. We might meet other women there, a whole group of them—and together we could make this place bigger than it was. Nearer to the house, I saw a woman working in the fields. She was large and sturdy, not much older than myself, with fire-colored hair and a dress that stretched like a rag over her hips. Wiping her hands from the dirt, she left prints on her lap, so often she seemed covered with her work—a stone of a woman, her hands sun-spotted and rough, her fingers short, nothing delicate, much like the house.

"Hard work," I called out.

"Always is." She raised her head, studying the shawl around my shoulders before she pulled back her chin.

"We're neighbors," I said. "First time in three years I've seen someone in this house. Our place is just over there."

"I've seen it," she said. "A big place." She lowered her head again.

I rubbed my neck. Inside that dim little cabin, I imagined her holding out a cup of water that sweated against its glass, cold as I believed I had not tasted for months, and offering the last piece of fruit from her pantry. I waited for her to invite me in, searching down the road for any kind of distraction—for miles there was little more than corn and beans.

Finally the woman straightened. "Enidina," she said. "We've been here only a few weeks. Haven't had the time to meet neighbors."

She was clearer to me when she stood, heavier and taller than I might have guessed, her speech coarse, impatient, but there was a carefulness in the way she moved. Dirt stained her stomach more than the rest of her dress, as if she could not help but touch the place again and again—there it was, I thought, a second life, something I often sensed in women before they even knew it themselves. I wanted only to cross that distance, to touch a bit of that softness and have it for my own. I reached out my hand, but it dropped dumbly between us. "Why, you're carrying," I gasped.

Enidina grimaced. She brushed her hand over her stomach again, as if to sweep away the dirt and everything with it. For decency's sake and luck's, I should never have let the words out. Later, I would think of what I said when Frank grew sick, when Enidina abandoned herself with such recklessness to the storm. What kind of woman was she after all—bent to the ground, her fingers thick as rope? I would never be as marked by this place or as raw, and even then I believed such a woman could never carry a child for long.

"My first," Enidina offered, though she seemed pained to say it. "I wouldn't be out walking for too long in this weather. It'll cook you through. That house of yours, it looks big enough to keep a woman busy I'd think. I'd think with a house like that, a person wouldn't have much time for visiting at all."

I opened my mouth, but already she had bent to her work, tearing weeds from the soil. What new low had this woman driven me to? I turned at once, heading in the opposite direction from home. When I looked back, she stood as if abandoned in her field, her hand on her forehead to hold off the sun as she watched me go, and I was not surprised when she called out. "I suppose I'll be seeing you," she said.

The road ahead was empty and behind me were only men and work closed off in a too large house I could never keep clean. My mother would arrive to care for the boys, chores would be taken care of for at least a day or so, and I could be gone, if only I could keep walking. The farmland was plain and forbidding—up ahead, not a living soul waited for me. What I wanted felt like a hunger, rising from my ribs, my throat, starved for something immense, golden. Jack was greater than many a man, but he could give me only sons and mud and butchered meat—I wanted something clean.

Enidina's house had disappeared behind me, but a small white chapel rose ahead out of the fields. I had lived in this place for years, but the chapel seemed new, standing as it did over the flat, graying bottomland and pointing upward, endlessly—as if it had nothing to do with this place and never would.

I moved in a daze by the time I opened the doors to that church. The very creaks in the floor welcomed me, the light through the windows stained and surreal, with a life and color all its own. Aisles of red carpet led like arrows to the pulpit, the wood painted white, and a heavy cross hung from above, glinting. I closed a communion glass in my hand and felt its cool weight, no chips, no stains—it shone with the candles that adorned the altar, all of them flickering under some unknown breath. The chapel resounded with footsteps. A tall, very pale young man in a dull gray suit walked down the center aisle, a limp in his stride, but the name I thought I heard from his mouth was my own. "Mary," he said.

I dropped the glass, but it did not break. It did not utter a sound when it fell. A cry escaped my throat, my name echoing against the walls in the voice of this stranger, and I felt myself lift. Here was a room of surrender and warmth. In this chapel I could do nothing wrong—and this man with his gentle limp, he was a part of it. A presence opened inside my chest, as if I were attended by thousands, and I knew at once I could carry this lifted-up feeling even if I returned home. I could keep this strength, drift above the rest. I could do my work without dirtying a finger, shake my husband's wildness out of him, and if I cared, if I was good enough—and I was determined to be—I could make that Enidina into the woman I had once imagined she was.

The man stood, waiting, and I wondered where I might have met him before or whether the sound of my name had come from some other place or time. "Miss?" he said. With his hands clasped against his stomach, he seemed the very picture of patience. Long and thin his hands were, like a woman's, but tufts of hair darkened his knuckles. He took my arm and sat me in a pew, his suit worn at the knees and his belt missing a loop, though his shirt was clean and white and tucked at his waist. "This is my father's church," he said at last, but I did not see a father about. It did not seem the place for fathers or old men, as his father would have to be—it did not seem the place for relations at all.

"My father built this church," he said.

"You don't have anyone else? A wife? A child?"

He looked at me puzzled. "No," he said. He sat very still then with his hand on my arm and did not speak. I could not remember when he had placed his hand there, but it was firm and hummed with a kind of electricity. I had never known a man to be so quiet, so closed in on himself, and I listened to him breathe. "Are you all right?" he said at last.

"It's your church," I announced. I had meant it as a question, but I wanted to believe it myself so let the end of my sentence drop. The man shifted his weight to see me—there in the slow turn of his mouth, in the rush of blood to his cheeks, he showed such a wonder at my presence that I felt reborn. He seemed a man who needed taking care of, and in the months and years that followed I would learn this was what drove his church members to him, slowly at first and then by the dozens. When after minutes he removed his grip from my sleeve, it left a damp stain. Later, when I would see him lift Enidina and the others from the lake, when he would bless them with a touch of his palm, I would recognize a different kind of strength.

This is what I'm trying to say, that goodness has its fire too. There are those who work for a living, who milk and slaughter and plow, and those who ready themselves for a different life—I was to be the second kind.

III

Enidina
(*Fall 1918–Fall 1919*)

The war's end found us in our bed. It was just before sunrise
on the eleventh of November, 1918. We heard the whistles
blowing in town, six miles away. With his eyes open to the
ceiling, Frank lay awake and whispered. "I just bet it's the
war. The war is over."

But the fields were the same. The houses and town, little changed. It was an easier season than we'd had in years
past, but not easier by much. My brothers had escaped the
call, and the local boys they'd lost were few and unknown
to us. Their pictures hung in the town market, stiff in their
uniforms. You may not understand, but an ocean lay between us and that war. We had sensed a kind of trouble. But
with our work from the early morning dark until evening,
we couldn't give it much thought unless we went to town.
The shops played Wilson's speeches on the radio, and we
listened with our neighbors. Still, we couldn't imagine such
distance, couldn't believe how men survived it in their ships.

"We're not from over there any more. None of us," my
mother had said once. "All of you have been born right here.
We're from nowhere but this place."

That spring and summer we grew apples, peaches, and
strawberries as we'd always done and ate much of what we
picked before dark, canning the rest. We worked from hand

to mouth, never letting what we had grown fall to the ground or be eaten by dirt. In the early morning, the chicken whose neck I broke with a snap of my wrist I would clean and dress for supper that very night. We often ate in the daylight then, the last of the sun grazing our plates. At the end of those months, the bacon and beef we'd dried were already gone. That chicken became a pale cut of meat between our teeth, as dull to the taste as cotton. When finally the corn and potatoes came, late as they were in the season, they were sweet and crisp and filled us while they lasted.

Even when we could hire hands, that was the way it was. The flies were thick about the kitchen. Mice ran the boards beneath our feet. Our house thinned and heaved in the late night winds. With the windows open, we grew used to the lack of stillness, a dusting of pollen on every last piece of wood. I was busy canning most days, a line of jars on my kitchen table. What tasted good and fresh in the early morning could turn my stomach by midafternoon. My fingers swelled with the juice, and the fruit bruised no matter how much care I took. I dropped the jars to boil in the kettle on the stove, tightened the lids once the fruit had set. All that effort and we wouldn't see those jars again until the weather turned cold, the glass dark, stored away in the cave we'd built in our yard.

The cave, that's what you might call a cellar now, though it didn't sit beneath the house. It was a hole we dug in the yard, deep and wide and lined with bricks. We covered it with a narrow wooden door and a mound of dirt as high as you are standing. It held those jars of fruit, vegetables, and meat as well as the cider and milk we hoped to keep for a time. My family had such a cave when I was young. It was a place the weather didn't touch. A place where as children we would play king of the mountain, the soil black on our knees. But underneath that mound, I couldn't tell it apart from a grave and I never went inside alone. Something in the cave was precious. For all we knew, time beneath that ground had stopped. My boy, sometimes I dream I'm down there still, what with the length of the days as I lie in this bed. At night the trees scratch the windowpanes. The air aches with so much silence, and it's dark as rot in this room, as if my eyes weren't open. I think I've already quit this place. But when a cow calls from a distant farm, as clear as if it fed on the grass outside, I know I'm just wishing. On the hottest nights, Frank swore he could sleep in the cave and keep just as well for the harvest in the fall. I slapped his hand to even kid as much.

Now with your grandfather gone, I think about the way that cave seemed to hold all of us in its grip. Every bit of food that kept us through the winter we locked beneath its door. If it vanished all at once, what would have become of us? You would never know it, but in our yard that cave still sits, empty but for the jars I left behind when I closed up a good half of this house. And soon this house will be empty too. *I hope you're well,* your mother wrote those eleven years ago, weeks before you were to be born. *And that you know I'm sorry for the way we left, but I wanted my boy born in another place.* Adaline never did give an address for writing back. I suppose she didn't want to hear what her leaving did. *The doctor says a month more,* she wrote. *But I know he'll be early. I dropped a penny as you always said and it landed on the fifteenth of November. That'll be the date, I swear.* After I'm gone, I hope these pages mean something to you. I don't have a hold on those years the way I once did, though they're more real to me than any of the days since. I've asked the nurse they send from time to time to be sure to save this notebook. But she's a stranger to me and I'm not so sure she will.

It wasn't until a year after the war that I knew Mary had troubles of her own. It was late in September. The cold weather had come. The season was only beginning but in the winter months the world beyond our door would be lost to us. I know. I've seen it. Loneliness can make you do terrible things.

It was a time of dark mornings and fresh meat. Frank worked at the butchering without lifting his head, his arms high in front of him. The path of the knife in his hand was clean, unstopping. The fat he cut away fell in a mess at our feet. We were to butcher eight hogs that day and sell the meat of four of them, worth more after butchering than hogs brought in on foot. Frank swung about, his arms greasy to his elbows. The front of his shirt hung with hair and waste. I spoke of sausages, of real meat for supper. How I would prepare them that night in a skillet with a molasses gravy, a side of potato or beans if we were lucky enough. The gravy boiled up thick in front of us as he talked, the sausage skins puckering in the pan above the heat. We had started work in the morning, before we could quite see. The walls of our barn and washhouse colored while the sun rose.

Mary stayed in our house while Jack shared the butchering with us, as their family would share the meat. "I have something for you," she'd offered when first they came that morning. She looked nervous and faded, a bruise high on her cheek, and she pressed a sack of flour against her chest. My boy, I can't say I knew how to feel about her then, so sharp was the loss of my child and her part in it, no matter how innocent. It had been four long years since, but I felt a pinch whenever we met. With a sweep of her hair, she kept that bruise of hers hidden. Still, as I led her in, she fingered her cheek until she saw me looking. Now with the butchering in my hands, I smelled the bread she would bake rising on the table, fat with yeast. I knew the warmth it promised. I kept an eye on our windows as we worked. Mary peered out at times but never joined us, my fingers full of filth.

I'd raised a fire first and started a large barrel of water for scalding. It would be some time before the water was right. Before it was hot enough to clean the hogs, but never so hot it cooked the meat. Nothing gets them so clean. This is how you do it. You dip your finger in three times. You count out slow: one, two . . . and on three, if the water is ready, it will burn before you can take your finger out again. Frank shot the hogs in the dark, and the noise of the gun broke against us. It seemed too early in the season to begin this work. The ground was muddy from summer and the cold unsettled. But I'd started the water and we were hungry.

Jack pulled the hogs up with the block and tackle and stuck them so they bled from the throat. Below him, Frank squatted with his face turned, holding the buckets that would catch the blood. He kept his eyes on the water as it warmed.

"They bleed better in a warm fall," Jack began. That knife was sure and powerful in his hands. We answered him by dropping our heads. The sun was rising and would soon grow bright.

"It would be better with sons, I think." Jack looked at me with this. The ground at my feet felt warm from the fire but damp with wet. My arms ached as he spoke. I remembered the stone marker for our firstborn. It stood beside our house. Kept as best I could from the weeds, it was well out of sight. "To help us, I mean," he went on. He always went on. "They're just boys, Mary thinks. Left them to sleep. And there she is, keeping herself in the house away from all this mess, or so she calls it. Shame to have this work and no one to see the way it's done."

"Sons would be more . . . ," I started to answer, but left it at that. Sons would be more to feed, I'd thought.

"You have to start with boys when they're young," Jack started again. "Before they get other curiosities. You have to set them right. Raise them to know the work." Jack grew quiet. His arms settled at his waist. I thought of Mary, at work in her house and always cleaning. She kept her boys in line, tried to wrench the farmer out of them. The first time she stood in our fields, I believed she'd left some bad luck at our place. Now through the open windows, I could hear her singing, high and strained, as she baked in our kitchen. "She's the only friend for you in miles," Frank had said. "I bet you're more alike than you think." But her husband sure was different. Jack stared now at the belly of the hog before him, working his jaw while the animal bled out. "There isn't much pleasure in it this way," Jack said.

Frank talked about supper where he crouched, about the steam in the kitchen, our table and his chair. "Did I ever tell you about Eddie's father, Jack? His favorite dog took sick once, gone to skin and bones. Wouldn't make a sound but to whine. I knew her dad would be upset about it. But what did he tell me when I asked? That his wife had made him a roast for supper. He listed what she cooked for him as if he was starved and could taste it right then, the side of pork, beans, and fried onions. It took a good fifteen minutes until he was done with it. And there I was, nodding my head. You knew he was talking about that dog the whole time, telling me how much he liked it, how much he'd miss it if it went. It was the way he said it, see? That dog was a mangy mutt. It barely moved from the corner of their porch except to lift its head. But I think it heard how Dad went on and got good and hungry. Went right for the scraps they'd left him, first time it'd eaten in days. Would you believe it? That dog is still with them, fattest animal I've ever seen."

Jack laughed, the body of the hog turning in front of him. "That's every man I've ever known," he said.

It was a fine sound to hear Frank go on, a fine way that water turned to steam beneath my hands. We tossed the hogs in one at a time, and the water jumped, wetting the ground around the barrel. They floated, turned on their backs, and we fetched them out again. Our hands grew red and wrinkled. Cooling our fingertips in our mouths, we could taste the hog and the muck it had lived in. Frank and I scraped the hides, the hair salting the ground a fine, white color, and he swept the back of his hand under his nose.

It didn't make Frank sick, this work, only restless and singing to himself. He tried to remember the words of a song and where the words were to rise and fall. It was strange to see a man so stained with grease sing this way. Strange how it lifted me from the work at my feet.

Jack cut along the length of the belly, letting the innards spill from the wound. We shared in scooping out the rest with our hands. Beginning at the head, we ran our arms deep into the body, the stench rising from under our fingers as we loosened the stomach, the intestines, the weak fat around the liver. It all dropped to fill the barrels at our feet.

Frank looked at the gutted skins where they hung and he stopped his singing. It was high in the day by then. The sun was sharp against the hides, turning them pink, limp. The sweat on his skin made Frank nearly transparent. He felt bloodless, he said, and swung on his feet. I saw this in him even before he spoke, his face hollowed out by the end of the summer months. He said he was hungry. It had been two long seasons since he'd tasted the like.

We had raised this meat, seen it birthed, give birth, seen it eat our feed and whine when it was hungry. Had watched it walk, fatten, warm itself in filth. We had raised it to be used. We took it to the feeding trough and forced it to eat, forced the mother to feed her young as they lined up against her belly. They sucked at her while she slept.

We spoke always of eating when we butchered, list-ing the foods that came to us with the seasons. We could remember the flavors of every meal, the last time we had known a pear, apples, or jelly. The changing textures of our gravies. We whispered our favorites to one another, speaking all in a rush . . . *Fried potatoes, sausages, hot noodles, corn bread, and eggs. Green beans cooked in onion, laid beneath a slab of bacon, creamed corn, and peas my mother made, served high on a plate. Warmed in the pot all day so you couldn't see what it was. Run together in a stew, in a juice, sauces and all of it dripping. It tasted like the only food you should ever want to have. My mother too, it's a wonder. It's a wonder what some women know . . .*

It was late in the morning by the time Mary came out from our kitchen, carrying her biscuits and glasses of lemonade on a tray. She wore my apron, a dull rag white with flour and tied about her twice. She looked right pleased with herself. As she made her way across the yard, the tray trembled in her hands. The air was chilly. The grass wet her shoes. She was close enough to us by then that I could see a sudden strain in her face, her eyes flickering.

It was the stench that struck her first. The smell of butchering is thick and bitter, strangely sweet. It clings to the skin. We smelled the same, the stink of our sweat as we worked. With the heat of the sun against us, our clothes steamed. Mary set the tray on the ground and cupped her nose. When she opened her eyes again, she saw us drenched in grease and blood over our fronts and arms up to our shoulders.

"Oh now." Jack grinned, rocking on his feet where he crouched. "It's not as bad as that."

Mary took a step back, wiping her eyes. "I baked these biscuits," she started.

"Oh now." Jack grinned at her. The early morning had been quiet. Close to stillness. The work had been easy with three of us at hand. Now Jack seemed to liven at the sight of his wife and the filth she hated, and he caught her against his chest. "Jack," Frank said. Mary cried out herself, trying to wrench away. Jack wouldn't let go, drawing her face against his neck and spinning her about, as if dancing. I remembered how he'd clutched his knife earlier in the morning, how swiftly he'd cut, his eyes on the hogs as they bled out. It went on too long, the way he held Mary with the same strength. She beat him with her fists.

Finally Jack stepped away. Mary's dress and hair were covered with waste. It clung to her wetly. She spit grease from her lips and straightened the apron over her skirt. "I brought these," she sputtered. "They're fresh." I thought well of her for trying to take it as she did, her chin quivering. "Oh now," Jack said. He rubbed his neck as we stared at him and then he turned away. I took one of the napkins Mary had brought, dunked it in our water bucket, and set to washing her face. Mary keened, bending at the waist and holding out her arms.

"Hush," I said. "We'll get it off." I found Jack out of the corner of my eye and he mumbled, stamping back to his place. Soon he was bent against the skins again and cleaning them with his knife. I licked my thumb and washed the most stubborn stains from Mary's cheeks. Still she shuddered. Her bruise had darkened since the early morning, the size of a fist. I would not touch it. "Hush now," I said again, tender this time. In my hands she felt as soft and frail as a child.

"That wasn't right of him. Not at all," Frank said. Now in the evening, he had walked into the kitchen smelling of soap, his back sloped, eyeing the stove where I worked. I shut my eyes and tried to shake away the thought. Frank's skin was red from scrubbing, the kitchen full with me and my work to feed him. My hands felt swollen and heavy, my figure too large in that place with the night coming in, the fire from the stove and a single lantern on the table. Frank kept his gaze on the frying pan where the sausages smoked.

"What do you think causes a man to do such a thing?"

"Meanness," I said. "Plain meanness."

Frank hummed in agreement and drew a chair from the table, sitting hard. We shook our heads. It was so strange a deed we couldn't think to say more. The heat from the sausages rose from the pan, the spicy scent turning through the room. For days that smell would be inside our clothes. Frank didn't move. When I turned from the pan, he looked through me, hungry for the tender meat in my hands.

I placed three large sausages on each of our plates and spooned gravy along their lengths. We sat with our heads bowed, the smoke warming our faces. Frank whispered to his breast. "Amen."

We ate quickly. Our jaws sore, our mouths rarely closing, licking our lips. We sat bowed over our plates across from each other with few words between us. I thought of

Mary and that bruise on her cheek, the way she'd tried to quiet herself. She'd lifted her tray from the ground after I'd cleaned her, scowled at the lemonade that drifted with dirt and grass. Finally she pushed the tray into my arms and walked off home. When I came back into the house, I saw she'd scrubbed our kitchen clean, and I hadn't had the time to thank her for it. The rest of the biscuits sat on my counter. None of us could eat them. Not yet. When Jack went after her, he walked clear of her swinging arms and didn't say a word. I worried about her with that husband. I worried a great deal.

"Finished?" I asked. We sat at the table with our plates empty between us. The windows looked solid with darkness and I felt I knew nothing beyond that door and never would. The weather that moved over us came from a distant place. We couldn't expect much good from it. And the good man across from me, he was the only man I believed I'd truly known. Frank shook his head and stood to help himself to more sausages from the skillet and started on these before he sat, intent on his chewing. He stared at the table before him as his fork struck his plate, slipped into his mouth, and struck again. Shutting his eyes, he kept on, striking down, his hand tight in holding his fork and trembling. At last he scraped up the rest of the grease.

Frank squeezed the tips of my fingers and sat back in his chair with a slow smile. In his tiredness, he walked to the bed and stretched himself out. I sank into the mattress beside him and listened, his arms quivering as he slept. After all those years I knew the look of him at least. Knew his smell. And I knew he would never do what Jack had done, not for the world. I rested but felt my fingers labor on as they turned against my stomach. That afternoon I'd worked for hours at the sausages while Frank delivered the meat to the butcher in the next town. Bent over near the barn, I sat on a small stool and lifted my eyes to see the quiet of our house. Far off, the trees broke the horizon, the fields gray and unplanted. It would rain soon, I'd thought, and the rain might turn to snow. The house sat between the fields and the coming weather, the place seeming distant from me and far, far from the living. Birds circled the sky above my head and begged for scraps. I couldn't see the families who lived nearest us, not even the Morrows down the road.

That night as I fell asleep, I worked at the sausages if only in my head and heard the rainstorm set in. The wind and rain settled me. My hands stretched the entrails again, tied one end of each length and held the skin open. The skins were frail and clear, sticking to my fingers. I pushed the ground meat through to make a stout sausage link, tied it swiftly at the end and put it aside. Another empty skin then, the mound of spiced meat lessening. My arms grew tired as they held the work up close to see. Pieces of meat fell and stained my lap. When finally my hands grew quiet, they rested on my stomach and I felt a fullness there. A quickening to accompany me.

IV

Mary
(*Winter 1919*)

Just a few weeks into winter, the afternoons grew heavy, my work faded to a list of chores, and I walked alone every day to the chapel through the snow. That fall the church had received a piano of its own—a gift from a wealthy family in town. When I opened the lid, the strings shuddered in the frame, the keys cool to the touch, but when I pressed my fingers down, they sang. What would my father have thought? He had been one for simple living, for the time of day when the sun had fallen, still hours before dusk, and he could note the difference. My father had left the board he carved for my first piano at the foot of my bed, a poor replica wrapped in brown paper and string. That summer in 1919, we had buried him on the south side of a hill facing a stand of trees, my mother clutching a blue handkerchief to her mouth. The stone held both his and my mother's names, and this proved best as my mother would follow him within a year.

Now as I sat in the chapel again, the fields outside were a dull white plain. The snow showed little save the shadows of birds—but in these walls I had to close my eyes to hear so much. No one listened as I played. Even Minister Borden kept to his rooms, taken I suppose with his books and papers. Still the keys of that piano hummed, one note following another—all that time playing that board my father had given me and I never imagined such a sound.

"Hello?" I called out. I stopped my playing and listened. Footsteps echoed in the back hall. As it grew late, the afternoon had turned into evening, the candles I had lit on the piano dimmed until I could no longer see the page.

"I'd hoped to hear you play," Borden said, his voice faint. At the back of the chapel, he stood very still in the dark with only the white of his shirt showing, a draft from the doors behind him making a low whistling. "You didn't stop because of me, did you?" he asked. I shook my head, though he could not see me well enough to know it. The bench felt suddenly warm beneath my dress, the blood pulsing in my fingertips, and the whistling too grew quiet. I did not dare move until his footsteps faded away. The light was gone then and I played what I could from memory, the hair on my arms raised by the cold—if not for the darkness, I could have seen my breath.

"The way to goodness," Borden had said, "is one of sacrifice. He who sacrifices will have it a hundred times returned." He stood at the pulpit looking down at the meager gathering, old and young but mostly old, twenty in all scattered in the pews. Still, he seemed pleased with the attention, though I am certain no one understood a word he said—no one did, but for me. The others sat with their hands in their laps, the old ones with their chins to their chests, asleep in the wooden seats until the music began. I never looked anywhere but up. Every week Borden hesitated less, seemed less uncertain, and soon the pews filled. That is what the expression on Borden's face was, really—the way he nodded at his words and turned the page with the tips of his fingers—the radiance he wore was a mirror of my own, seeing him.

A week before Christmas, I crouched with Borden and the other wives in the church basement and for hours we fixed evergreens into yards of garlands and wreaths. Sacrifice, I thought, and the wreaths grew in a pile around my feet while theirs remained scattered with loose pinecones and needles, what with all their talk. "How are the boys?" they asked. They were plump about the ankles, their voices dense as cream.

"Your youngest, he's four, isn't he? That's a long while between them. I would think you'd want more for the farm."

I studied the one who had spoken. She lived in town, a wife of the man who owned the market, stiff and gawky as her name was—Mrs. Reed. She had pinned a flower of silk too close to her face, her hair a bush. I knew she had felt many a coin in her palm, the ring on her finger a prize. More children. But how could we? My husband came in late to our bed and lifted the blankets, his hand on my hip, but soon enough it slipped off as he fell asleep.

"My husband works very hard."

The woman smiled. "But still . . ."

"Still?"

"He's still your husband."

"Mrs. Reed," Borden said.

The woman let out a shout and stood, gripping her skirt. She had done nothing but hold the pine branches as she talked and the sap had gathered on her lap in a sticky pool.

"You'll need a good soap for that," I said.

Mrs. Reed looked at me. "Yes, I know dear. I know."

Borden dropped his head, reading from his book, and the others grew quiet. Mrs. Reed scrubbed at her skirt with her fingers until they turned the color of the wool, a sickly yellow-green, and she threw her hands in the air. "Are you coming?" she said to the others, gathering her belongings. The women gazed at her for a moment—with a quick nod they abandoned their work, stuffed their purses with needles and scarves, and tossed their coats over their shoulders— then they were gone. Save for the two of us, the church was empty then, a cold wind batting the window panes. I had no desire to join that wind any time soon, no matter what needed me at home—with Borden's quiet presence in the room, my fingers worked at fastening the pine needles with thread. He had seen, I knew, and he had come between me and those women.

"I thought you might play," he said after a time. "Since you're staying, I mean."

"What would you like to hear?"

"Don't ask," he said. "Everyone wit. their questions. Just this morning, old Craeger wanted to kn what he should do with his chickens. They'd gotten out of their pen into Peterson's corn. I tried to send him to the deputy in town, but the law, he said, he didn't trust it. 'What greater law was there than God's?'" Borden laughed, dropping his head.

"He's right."

"Who?"

"Craeger."

Borden studied me and stood from his chair. "Mary," he said. "You should have worn gloves." I looked down at my hands—my fingers were red and wet with cuts. Borden crouched next to me with a wince and took a handkerchief from his pocket, holding my fingertips tight. When he closed his eyes, I looked down at the top of his head where the part in his hair showed a delicate line of skin, my hands caught between his. The handkerchief was spotted with blood when he took it back.

I had seldom in my life known such ecstasy and fear, and never both at once, but as I made my way home through the high snow and wind, I did not feel a touch of that cold—how could this be anything but the work of a higher presence? I walked with my coat open and swinging around my legs, my scarf in my hand. The moon was high by the time I left him, the sky black as midnight, and snow drifted through the fences while the grasses hummed. Across the frozen plain, the earth woke to my footsteps. When at last I reached the door to my house, I believed I was as bright and clear as the snow itself, touching ground.

Over the next few weeks I woke to a certain kind of dullness. In the morning light, our room was narrow and pale. Jack set out early for his shift at the mill, work that put food on our table in the winter months, and I lay in our bed

listening to the clock on the wall and the sounds of day-
break. I felt an ache in every part of my person and was sick
of my own skin, how faded and thin and all-encompassing it
was, like a dress I could never take off. Outside the door, my
sons sulked for their mother, whispering just loud enough
for me to wake, and I smelled the sweat on my husband's
pillow. The morning after my visit to the church, Jack had
come in for his breakfast and found me at the stove, looking out our kitchen window. The barn stood dark against
the early light and a mist clung to the grass, easing toward
the house. "Mary!" Jack yelled—beneath my hand the sausages on the stove hissed with a heavy smoke, the pan gone
dry. Jack shoved the pan at me as I tried to push him away.
For days, a burn shone red in the tender skin between my
forefinger and thumb. Ever since, Jack had often lost his
patience with me, suspending a fist just before my face with
only weariness to hold him back. Lying in our bed, I shuddered to think just how long it would be before he struck
me again, and a blast sounded like a train coming at us, so
loud it shook the house.

I threw on my shawl and ran out to the road. A steam
boiler had once burst in the mill the next county over and
killed five of the men where they stood. Had Jack gone to
work as he did every morning? Was he there still? Despite
everything, it was Jack who kept our farm from starving—
and without him, the house would rot on its perch, the land
crawling out from under us, and my sons too young and
nearly useless at saving the place from the fate of the family
that had owned it before. "You'll be lost in such country,"
my mother had said on first seeing it. "It'll eat you alive

before you even know what living is." Now the birds overhead were calling, and the cold of the night weeks before returned to me, my visit to the church and back again—I had never in my life known such pleasure in the aching of my limbs. It was rising in me again, the hard beating in my chest and the feeling of deliverance—so relentless and shocking in its presence that I found myself running to the mill to escape it. I was no proper wife, I never had been, and now I hardly had the sense to stop moving, so sure was I in the churning of my stomach that something terrible had come to us and I was somehow to blame.

When at last I reached the mill, the saws had started up again and the walls shuddered. The men worked in overalls and goggles, indistinguishable in the half-light and coated in sawdust. They had heard it too, the crash breaking like thunder overhead. Shutting down the saws, they had stripped off their hats and stepped out to see—but the noise was gone, the fields unchanged. The foreman had insisted they start to work again, and the men shouldered the heavy logs. When they saw me standing there with my wet face and shaking, one of them signaled his hand in the air and the saws stopped at once. Out of the dimness, Jack pushed through the line of men and caught hold of my shoulders as if I might faint.

My husband may have seemed a brute, taller by a head and thicker than most, but in his size there was a hollow space just below his ribs that felt to the touch like tenderness. "Mary," he had said, and this only months after my second was born. "The house is something, isn't it?" He had said it with a look of wonder on his face, standing just across the yard in the night and staring up, his palms open. He wore the stench of a day's work on him, his shirtsleeves soggy in the heat and a streak of dirt across his forehead. I knew then I had done what he could never leave behind—I had filled this house for him, that was what he meant, and in that darkness, the house seemed a bright and restful place, if only for a while.

Now at the mill I clung to my husband and glimpsed that tenderness in him again, knowing at once he would never disappear from me in any kind of accident. "Go home," he whispered. "That noise isn't about us." Jack's breath was hot and sure against my skin, but it was not relief I felt— not yet. I could not for the life of me forget what had sent me running, but not even my fear of losing him would make sense of the dread that held more tightly to me now. So I left him to his work. I turned straight away from the mill with only a nod. Walking aimlessly in the open air, I thought about judgment, and soon I found myself running again, heading down the path I had beaten all those years between the Currents' house and our own.

Outside their barn, Enidina slouched against one of their horses, smoothing the animal's back. When the horse shook and ducked at my footsteps, her heavy hand seemed to quiet it, both of them raising their heads.

"I suppose you heard it too," she said.

"I thought we might take the wagon. Find out what it was all about."

The horse swung its neck, sinking its muzzle in Enidina's palm and snatching at a handful of grass. Enidina squinted at me and wiped her hand against her dress. "I suppose we should," she said.

We took their wagon and Enidina steered the horses in the direction the noise had come from. For miles we rode without a word and the wagon lurched and rolled, the wheels slipping on the icy road, but every once in a while she would twist her head and study me. "You're quiet," she said.

"Can't I have a little quiet for once?"

"Sure."

"Does it always have to be me talking? Every single time?"

Enidina faced front again, shaking her head. "That horse," she said at last and pointed her chin. "She's been strange for weeks now. Restless. I think one of the males' been at her. Act the same as people, they do." Enidina left off, and only then did I notice how the horse before us swayed and strained as she pulled.

"If you know animals, you can always tell," she went on. "At least I could. What do you think?"

"The horse?" I started. "She seems well enough." Enidina squinted at me again and I tightened my coat.

"Well, I'll be," Enidina swore. From the fields ahead of us, a smell of burning drifted and smoke rose from the prairie, the air wavering over a wide strip of land. Enidina snapped the reins until the horses burst into a gallop and I covered my nose. The windows of the houses we passed lay shattered on the ground, their curtains blowing outside the sills. From an empty door, a smoke-colored mutt sprang as if rabid, barking at us from the ditches. The road had filled—wagons and men hurried along on foot, eager for a ride, all of them heading toward the smoke and heat with fear in their eyes.

Then it was before us. The prairie was afire—a good acre or more of it, without source it seemed, for the land itself was isolated and barren, without a single building or tree that could have burst and ignited the ground. The snow had melted a good distance, but the grass around the fire remained untouched, as if the flames had dropped from the sky. Enidina tied the horses and we ran out to see. Along the outskirts, a crowd stood, blackened with ash from head to toe. Others sat on the ground, having watched for hours while the seats of their trousers grew wet with snowmelt.

That was the way it was, the old watchers quiet with waves of newcomers coming in—and with them, rumors spread like a fever, so while the fire cooled, the crowd heated. It was a boy's trick, some said. It was an accident, said others. "I saw it myself," a man yelled. "A rock fell from the sky. It burst in the air." Others cried in agreement, said they had seen it too—it broke the glass in their windows for miles around. The crowd jeered, chattering nonsense. In their midst, a woman still heavy with birth and milk stood dumb with her infant, ignoring its wails. Her face was colorless, her shoulder soaked with drivel. The child itself was red-skinned and crying, a furious body in its mother's arms—its cries shivered through the air. At last a voice shouted, "It was a sign from God."

I looked up into the sky. My tongue tasted sour and black, the smell of burning meadow. Next to me, Enidina stood with her legs wide, watching the others more than the charred prairie itself and me more than anyone else. When a sob rose from my throat, she took my arm in her terrible grip. "This here is nothing," she whispered. "This is just natural. Best we don't look for reasons at all."

I wrenched my arm away. The baby's wail grew. All around us were farmers and wives staring into the blackness, and I knew God had come. I saw His face looking down at me from the very clouds. There was no place He wasn't—and worst of all there were places He was without question, and no heavy hand was going to keep the world from trembling. I left Enidina where she stood and I stumbled forward into the backs of strangers—they parted like grass to let me go on. Before me the land had been touched by greatness and I threw myself into it, surrendering myself to that fertile ground. The arms of forgiveness gathered me in, a warmth rising from the cold, and I let myself go numb.

It was then I slept—and in that sleep I imagined myself sitting in an empty pew at the back of the chapel. The air shone through the windows with a yellow haze that warmed my lap, so different from the light that left the fields in their pale coating of dust. The rest of the chapel had fallen into darkness, not a sound from the back hall, and I pressed my forehead into my hands. Out of the shadows a boy came and stood at my feet, blocking out the light. He was restless and smelled of smoke, all muscle and bone as some boys are just before they turn men, and in his fist he held a bloody handkerchief—as I watched, that handkerchief grew to the size of a sheet and I shielded my eyes.

When I was young, I had found such a light in an opening of the woods. The trees broke, leaving a wide stretch of grass where I could lie on my back and let the narrow shaft of sun hold me in its grip. I had escaped my mother's house for a few moments of peace and found this place where I was hot-skinned and drowsy, the center of all I could see. Lying there, I believed something was beginning—it was something I believed I should feel ashamed for, but didn't, and as I slept after that fire I felt that beginning again. The boy stood in the chapel at my feet, but now such a pleasure rose in the core of my stomach—quick as a liquid that would keep me swollen for months—and I knew I could hold on to that feeling as if holding on to a very bright light.

When I woke, I lay in the same narrow bed where the day had first found me. The windows were dark with evening and a doctor held my wrist. Jack paced the far end of the room, and I felt a sudden affection for him, for the weight of his shoulders and his sullen footsteps, the fear I could see in his dirt-stained fingernails as he swept back his hair—how long had it been since I had done the same? My run from earlier in the afternoon seemed strange to me now—I had never disappointed him, never in our marriage had I imagined another life.

But there was Enidina. She stood in the corner with that same maddening look of patience she always wore, and the muscles in my legs ached, a knot in the back of my neck. I knew what had happened then, with a pinch in my chest I knew it—I had fainted on that ground and Enidina had carried me home. Only when Jack bent to touch my cheek did my calm return, his heat and size so easily obliterating her presence. "What's wrong with her?" Jack asked the doctor, but the doctor only shook his head. The light shifted. Enidina's face appeared above my husband's shoulder and she opened her mouth. "She's carrying," she answered. "And who knows what else."

V

Enidina

(*Winter 1919–Spring 1920*)

———————

A full house, my mother wrote of her Christmas. *The little ones played in the yard while Sarah helped me with the meal. Eight they number in all with this new one. I never thought I could survive grandmothering alone, but I dare say I see your father's face in every one. Try to forget is what they tell the mothers who lose them. Now every one is carrying a young thing on her shoulders, though she'd never have dreamt it. Enidina, you've got to have faith in that if you're ever to have another child.* I finished my mother's letter and read it again, the paper worn. My boy, if I could tell my mother now what losing is, she'd never have thought a person could be so easily replaced. Not at my age, at least. In those early years, I kept my mother's letters in a bundle beneath our mattress, tied with a string, and I read each one through again until I received the next. I missed my brothers. Hadn't seen the new niece, though she was several months old. At Thanksgiving, we'd sat around as we once did and told stories, the men with guitars on their hips. We weren't the most religious of families. Save for holidays we didn't go to church. Still, we had a hold on right and wrong, one that had been passed down to us over the years. We had faith in humility and kindness, and when we sang the Lord's Prayer we knew every part. Hearing that, it was the fullest I'd felt in some while. But the distance wasn't such a little thing then. More than eight hours it took by wagon, and one way at that. It was too long to leave the cows without hiring help. Just before Christmas, the smell of the air warned of snow, making the trip longer still.

I'd picked a stranger for a husband, someone from outside the neighboring towns, but he seemed to know me the first day we met. Mind you, I never did wish for anyone different. Even so, those wagon rides between my home with Frank and the place I was born left us sore, so stiff was the board we sat on and the wheels ill suited to the broken tracks. It was hard for either of us to sit in one place for long. We were used to work. Used to a warmer kind of ache when we went to bed. We had to mind the weather, for fear the wheels might stick or the horse sicken herself with damp. We carried blankets to keep us from the cold. When at last we came to my mother's house, my brothers rushed to meet us, gripping the tender bones in our backs. We had changed in our looks and ways more than the children, they said. In that place, I felt like a child again myself.

With that letter once more in my hand, it was now well after New Year's and I was growing big again. Already I planned to write my mother that she should have another grandchild in mind. I'd gotten sick on so many mornings, but was set on keeping myself full with any ready food. For Christmas, Frank had bought us fancy plates, plates for more visitors than we would ever need. They were a delicate gift, packaged in dusty newspapers. The papers spoke of the war though the war was a year over. When I tore them away, the plates underneath were the brightest yellow I'd seen.

Finer than anything I'd held before in my hands. I'd wrapped them up quickly, storing them in the pantry for a time when I wasn't afraid of using them. Now with a bucket of water hot on the stove, I soaked the new dishes.

I'd spent the early hours bringing wood into the kitchen and piling it by the stove. The walls of the kitchen crowded in as I fed the fire, but soon it burned well enough alone. The house at my back seemed hollowed out, the cold breaking against the windowpanes. The child I carried strained with the work in my hands. I took the plates out of the water and they seemed far too delicate, the twelve of them thinner than my fist when stacked together. Having those plates, I thought our life might be growing toward something, being of use as they were and beautiful too. How both came about at once, I didn't know. The plates steamed as they dried on the table, but still there was dinner to make. A meal for Frank when he returned from work of his own. I dropped in the last of the wood and my stomach turned, an ache in my chest and throat. A wave of dizziness took me. As I gathered the plates together, they chattered and dripped. When I tried to lift the stack, they slipped from me and a wetness broke from between my legs. The kitchen table rose above my head, the fire in the stove blazing. The plates shattered, the floor beneath me suddenly wet and my skirts soaked as I fell into the mess.

I could not think to stand but stayed on the floor, sick of myself. My legs lay heavy in front of me, my red, wearied hands in my lap. I wasn't enough of a woman to carry a child, not enough of one to do what was most natural. Next to me the wood popped in the stove. I thought of the fire I'd seen in the fields, the way it seemed to drop out of nowhere. I'd already felt the sickness of this child in my stomach then, but I'd had my doubts. I lifted the stove's lid to brighten the room, and the iron burned my skin. I wondered at the floor, the soiled insides of our house. Our boots had brought the mud in and now there was the sickly sweetness. There was no good time for cleaning it. The little sun in our rooms and the heavy work had helped keep the dirt hidden from us. But as I rested there, it was plain to see. I didn't have the life in me to scrub the floor as I should. I knew only the shame of it and the reddish stain that grew in my lap, knowing what that stain was.

It was then I imagined Mary. At our kitchen window she stood looking out, rubbing her knuckles into the small of her back. Bent under her own weight, her stomach swelled inside her dress. When she stepped over me to reach the stove, her skirt swept my face. She washed her hands in the bucket and it was a long time she was washing them, her ankles bloated and her heel close to my wrist. I laid my finger on the crown of her foot and felt the fine bones there.

"Mary," I said, looking up. "You have such easy children. So many." She answered by lifting her hands and flicking her fingers until my cheeks burned with the drops. When she stepped off, out of the kitchen, I was left. The bucket atop the stove was boiling, spitting water on my face. My finger rubbed at notches in the floor.

Outside, the animals in the barn were calling for their meal and I knew I was late for them. I feared I would be late several hours more. I imagined myself at my regular chores, carrying buckets. The feedings were a gray time, in the early morning and the hours just before dusk. The animals would rush me, their whiskers wet. If I wanted, I could pour one of the buckets in the trough and leave the other in a closed-off stall for the weaker ones. When I was tired, I tended to do such a thing. They had a way of marking time, those feedings. I'd broken a path from the house to the barn with all my walks between.

So many days I worked in the house and felt the animals in the rooms behind me. In the kitchen, I heard them cry, imagined them breaking through the roof overhead. If I'd pressed my hands into the corners of our house, the sound of all their wanting came in. Their smell. The chaff on their skin. They wanted to eat from us, the animals. They wanted always to eat and they were eating us. My hands ached from carrying buckets. My days were taken up with the work.

"We can't be drowned," my mother had said to Frank. "None of us." This I'd heard after the loss of our first child. I could hardly believe it even then. "We crossed the ocean for this land," she said. "We were born, every one of us, with the caul over our heads."

My boy, this place isn't what it used to be. It was always difficult, but still it bore some life. No old women in their beds. I was always the hearty kind. I thought I could live alone for years more than that woman down the road. It's the thought of seeing your face that keeps me writing. Still, it pains my hand to give out so much.

Without knocking, the nurse invites herself in with her black leather bag and her hair pulled back with pins. She is thin and pale and walks as if she knows this house, her voice much too quick. There's something in her seriousness, in the way she seems ready to jump out of her skin.

"Who sent you?" I ask.

"County services," she says, but she's slow in saying it. I know her voice, but I can't place it.

"Whose?"

"The county."

"Services for what?"

She wears a smile like your mother's, cocked at the corner of her mouth. I've asked her this same question every day now and I'll keep on asking it until she gives an answer that makes sense. "Why don't you let me worry about what services, Mrs. Current?" she says. "Why don't you just let me get started."

I study her, but let her be. I don't have energy for visitors. As much time as these pages are taking, today and the day after that are the least of my worries. The nurse carries in buckets of water from the kitchen and strips the sheets. I know the song she hums. A lullaby. The same Mary and I once sang to our own. When she rolls me on my side, my breasts and belly drop like sacks of grain and I'm not so sick I can't smell the difference. I was never proud of my own skin, but it didn't used to look so mean. My ribs show and the flesh hangs from my hips. The water is warm. That sponge in her hand pulls at me until I wince. Not since I suffered baths as a child in my mother's kitchen have I let another person do what I've done my whole life. "You know," the nurse says. "You could get out of this bed if you wanted. You've got nothing wrong with you except being good and tired." Her voice moves the way of her hand, warm like that and circling. But the air after she's finished bites.

I pull the blankets to my chin, but she tells me to wait. I remember my hand wet on the small of your mother's back, trying to keep her still in our washbasin. Such a wail she put out, that curly hair of hers a nest. *Got work canning in a factory*, your mother would later write, from Des Moines that time. *Men's work, but so many have gone to war, I don't mind it a bit. Out of the sun all day and such a din.* Your mother and her letters. She wrote only a handful for me to keep under my mattress all these years. Never so much as I wrote my own. When she was young, your mother once came in with a ruddy dust on her hands and feet, holding up those hands as if she carried something delicate, so red I thought they were bleeding. I asked her where she'd gone. "The railway," she said, looking at her skin. "What kind of place has dirt like this?" Those trains, I knew, they must have carried that strange soil in with them. But I didn't know what those places were myself. For weeks after, Adaline talked about red-colored grass and the children who might play in it, their skin flushed as if they'd been out in the sun too long. A different kind of life, she must have thought.

I let the blankets go and the nurse gives her crooked smile. When she starts to work again, her touch is faint enough, I can almost keep my eyes from tearing. It was more than a week ago when she first came, and I woke to find her in my chair. When I opened my eyes, she held up her hand as if to ward me off and she called me by my name.

"Listen," I said. "I don't take to strangers. Especially the kind who make themselves at home."

"All right," she answered, dropping her hand.

"No it's not all right. Not in my house." The words caught in my throat, a fog over my eyes. I reached out to clear it, but the woman never went away.

"So," she said, looking around the room. Her nose twitched. She didn't seem to know what to do with herself. "If that's the way you're going to be." She clapped her hands and went off at once to my kitchen, marching back with a mop and duster under her arm. I have a small room in the front of this house. The bed takes up most of it. I've lined family photographs five deep in front of my dresser mirror, all facing my pillow. The nurse must have polished every frame, studying her face in the mirror as she did. Sometimes I found her studying me. When finally she left, the picture of Mary's youngest stood alone out front, as if that child were one of ours. Years ago, I'd thought he was.

My boy, I may tell you things that are difficult to know. I am not always proud. There are times in this life when a person suffers from the ways of others. And there are times when a person does a terrible wrong, if only because she can't see through to anything else. I'll try to remember what I can, but I fear I'm writing to ghosts. I used to believe I might find you. I wandered the streets of town hoping just that. This was harder to do once the town had grown. With all the houses on Main, we might be up to a few hundred now, if not more. I don't know the use in so many of us living so close. And I don't trust the way I can stand in the square and not smell the cattle, even when the wind is up. Fair and black-haired, I believed you must be, like your mother and grandfather both. The year you must have turned five, I saw just such a child in town, an ice cream cone in his hand. "Come now," his mother scolded him. "It's going to waste." But that boy wouldn't take a lick, and he ducked from his mother when she tried to take it from him. I know how it is, I wanted to say. Trying to save what you cherish as much as that. And there he was, holding on to that cone while the chocolate ran in rivers down his arm. There was nothing he could do but watch.

I woke on that floor in a chill. The fire in the stove was close to dying, the room nearly black. I sat as if I'd always been sitting there. As if I'd been born in the place, feeling the break of that birth, the crying I must have done, and the shock of air against my skin. The animals sounded desperate in their stalls and I believed they would soon break out. They would be in the house soon, in the kitchen even. They would eat off me whatever they found.

I drew myself up and leaned against the stove, layering in what wood I could reach. Soon it was warm and light in the kitchen, and I dropped rags on the floor to scrub up the mess with my foot. I swept the shards of plates far into the corner and picked up the one plate that hadn't broken, darkly stained as it was and crusted now like my dress. Outside, footsteps crushed the gravel and I knew Frank had come. He would be wanting dinner. Something hot I could set out for him and take my place across the table, watch him eat while his day fell away.

In the evenings after helping his cousin, Frank came home quiet. He didn't much like the work at the mill. Still, we needed the pay and his cousin needed the extra man, if only two days a week. Often the sawdust so stung Frank's eyes that he came home near to blind. He missed the way our farm grew. The sound of being called for. Every farmer I knew felt the same, Jack and all the rest, but Frank felt it more.

I heard him then on the steps though I didn't want to. I had nothing for him. When he walked through the door, he brought in another layer of mud. He lifted a chair from our table, eased himself into it. I laid out a knife and fork, gave him a cloth to wipe his mouth, a toothpick for his teeth. I hadn't the time, you see. Not for any proper meal. I'd listened all day to the animals calling for food and my head was fevered. I held my stomach to rub away the cramps, felt I was rotting in my insides. Frank stared at the table before him, his eyes sore and lids heavy, close to sleep. The room was almost too dark for him to see. The animals too were quiet now and unforgiving. I laid the unbroken plate on the table and left him to his meal.

Sitting on our bed, I thought about cleaning. My dress was sour, the skirt still damp and sticking to my legs. I tried to listen to him and wondered if Frank was a lonely man. I wondered if he worried about me. From the kitchen, he let out a shout and his chair fell. This life I loved, it'd given me nothing to keep. I was sick of myself, sick of my good husband who I knew should expect more of me. The curtain that made for the door between the kitchen and our bedroom trembled. Frank stood on the other side, looking in. "Eddie," he whispered. Lying back, I knew I'd made a good mess of it. *We are drowning, Frank,* I thought. *No children. Nothing for years.*

VI

Mary
(*Summer 1920 – Spring 1922*)

My youngest came easy in the end, though carrying him
was difficult, with all the dreams and pain that I had. This
was my last—I knew it then—I had reached the age to put
such things behind. When he was free of me, I let myself
drift, broken only by his cries and feeding, a sleep that must
have lasted for days.

I had seldom before so lost track of time, but in that sleep
a certain shifting seemed natural, and any hold on the hour
or day of the week has remained loose in me ever since. I
could remember the warmth of my mother's hand holding
me when I was young and even the shape of it, blunted and
thin and already veined. What a strange sort of skin we
grow as we age, one that never forgets a single gash or
pinch or season out in the sun. My mother's hand was worn
along the knuckles, a nervous habit she had of rubbing
them. My own had already grown swollen from scrubbing,
my fingertips dull from playing my imagined piano along
any stretch of wood. Every misstep, it makes its mark. I
touched my son's cheek and it felt as smooth and clean as
an egg—whatever doubts and accidents would later trouble
him did not reveal themselves, not yet.

"Awake?" My husband crouched over me and I felt the
darkness shift—even in his sleep, his size took up our bed,

his shoulders and chest so heavy the mattress sank beneath his weight. At night the noise of his breathing grated on me, and when I closed my eyes the way the world seemed to tremble and dim seemed entirely his doing. When he eased himself against me, my stomach clenched. So soon?—my new boy was barely months in our bed. My husband raised himself up, the ache of his work releasing itself into me until my breath stirred, my hips rising as if remembering another life—it was another face I saw then, another skin, though I would not name it, could not let myself remember beyond a few weeks. My husband called my name, and when at last he burrowed his head into my neck, I brushed my fingers across his back, settling him.

When next I woke, Jack was quiet in our bed. The absence of his heavy breathing had brought me back to our room. My new boy lay asleep at my side, Jack rested on the other, but when I opened my eyes, I found my husband raised on his elbow, his head cocked in his hand. In the silence, he studied the both of us as if we were strangers in his bed.

That summer after I turned twelve, I went to the woods near my home nearly every afternoon to escape my mother's house. In that small space surrounded by trees, I plucked the grass around my feet and made a level plot for a blanket. The space was no larger than two sheds put together, the sun reaching the grass for an hour or more just after noon, and one day I found a scattering of animal bones in the brush. The animal was long-limbed with a heavy skull, all but the bone eaten away. It was simple-looking enough, no more than a pile of sticks, and I imagined piecing it together again until the animal lay fixed and whole on the grass. Who ever thought the making of life was such a complicated thing? For months my mother had warned me about the wrong kinds of dresses, dancing with a boy's hands on your hips, and the company I might keep, life leaping into me at a snap of a finger. "It happens easier than you suppose," she said.

In the woods I smelled smoke and turned on my stomach—a boy stood in the shadows behind the trees, watching me. He was from our school but several years older, lanky and muscle-thin, the smoke smell coming from his fingers. When he saw me looking, he raised a hand to me and walked off. Over the next few weeks, I caught the same smell, different from a fire, but close enough that I thought someone might be burning leaves in a nearby yard, and when I looked, the boy was there again, watching, leaving just as quickly. "Are you supposed to be out here, all on your own?" he called out at last. "You're in the sixth class, aren't you? The smart girl. But you're not so smart you don't look like something. Mary, right?" It was hot and the light shifted, the woods abuzz. This boy smelled the way the older ones sometimes did to a girl, musk and salt and cigarettes—an awful smell I have thought ever since. "You won't tell anyone, will you?" he said. "The way you're always out here, like you're looking for something on that blanket of yours. Anyway, you'd better not. Knowing who my father is. Knowing your father works for him." He stepped out from the trees and into my circle of sun, his boot kicking my blanket. When I reached out to straighten it, he caught hold of my arm and did not let go.

"My God," Jack had said the first night of our marriage. Lying together, he had lifted the quilt from my legs, and I snatched it back. Under the light of the lamp, the sheets looked spotless. Jack put his face in his hands and turned away.

"It's not the same with everyone," I said, steadying myself before I reached for him. "It doesn't mean—"

"I know what it means."

"But it's not—"

"It's plenty."

I sat up against my pillow and looked down at my lap, wet and sore as it was. My cheeks burned, and I lifted the sheet again, pinching the skin of my thighs until they turned red. I remembered the day I had met him and the violence in his voice, the way it thrummed inside me like a finger plucking a string. If I had a knife at hand, I might have cut myself just to give him that bloody stain he wanted, but it was too late. That boy in the forest with me, with his smoky weight and the crush of his legs—he had made it too late for a long time. I was the worst a woman could be and now my husband believed it too.

Over the next few years, Jack worked with a kind of desperation I had rarely seen in him. In the afternoon, I kept an eye on him in the fields, Kyle heavy in my arms. Already

Jack had cleared a broader patch of land to the east with the plow, but late one morning he decided to work back through with only his fingers and a rake, clawing up what the machine had missed. "Slow," he spat, watching our boys where they crouched in the rows behind him. "You're not to leave a single twig." Beneath the sun, the fields were deeply furrowed and wavering—my sons worked listlessly, close to the ground and trailing after their father. When finally Jack seemed to forget them, they stole back to the house and closed themselves in their rooms. They would not appear again until dinnertime, not a word in the kitchen as we ate. Still Jack worked on, breaking the skin of his knuckles against pebbles and sticks, his back bent, pouring himself out until he had left the soil gutted after him. There was a fever in the way he took to the land, and I watched and waited, unsure how long he would take to work it out.

When Jack came in at last to the kitchen, it was already dark and his hands were ragged. I took them in mine and hurried him to the wash bucket for soaking, fetching a roll of bandages I had waiting. In the corner, my youngest fretted in his basket.

"That boy," my husband whispered.

"What boy?"

"He's strange to me."

I kept at the bandages, wrapping them around my husband's fingers though my own felt faint. "What now? All that work has gone to your head. Kyle's still new to you, that's all. It doesn't make a stranger out of him."

I shook my head and tied the bandages, turning his hands so I could see them—they lay large and wounded in mine, trembling. Looking down at me, Jack stayed quiet, though his pulse raced. The room was still, that motor in Jack raging to a pitch—he tore his hands from my grip and I fell, catching hold of the table. The bones in my wrist cracked. "Jack," I called out, but he kept his back to me. Alone on the far side of the room, he stood red-skinned and bristling, the table sprawled on its side between us.

"So Eddie lost it," he spit out at last, hiding his face. "Frank says she's had an awful time. Sounds to me like she's doing things a person shouldn't do. Crazy things, sounds like." He stopped, righted the table, and swept his hands across the surface, wincing at the touch. "Best you go see her," he said. "At a time like this, women need women. Isn't that right?"

I rubbed at the pain in my wrist, and he wiped his mouth and went out. I thought of our boys, how they bounded down the stairs for their supper, all of them limbs and restlessness—so like their father. Kyle cried from his basket and my breasts ached. Out the window, Jack walked across the yard, lit now only by the lantern he carried, and he disappeared from me into the barn.

Up ahead, Enidina's house was quiet. Three Jerseys sat together in the grass against the barn fence, their tails kicking, and a cat dropped off the porch and chased an insect over the walk. Inside, the house was dark and still and smelled of sickness, but soon a wet metallic ticking sounded from the kitchen.

I found Enidina scrubbing the kitchen floor by hand. A pail of water sat at her hip, the water gray with mud and grass, but the floor was clean, the rag worn to threads. Enidina stayed on her knees, her face flushed. "Eddie," I whispered—only when Kyle let out a cry from my arms did she drop her rag and look up, blinking against the light of the open door.

"Is everything all right?" I asked.

She sat back on her shins, brushing her skirt. "All right," she said, eying the stiffness of my wrist as I held Kyle. Without another word, she drew herself to her feet and reaching into her cabinets took down two teacups and set the kettle to the stove.

"I have some crackers," she said without looking at me. "Something he can suck on." She dampened a towel with the kettle water when it warmed and laid the towel over my wrist, tying it close. I flinched but the towel numbed the pain and held my wrist tight. "I hope it'll do," she said.

We sat at their table and Enidina closed her hands around her cup and seemed to breathe it in, the steam wetting her cheeks—her knuckles were red and swollen, her fingertips puckered. I rested Kyle on my knee and she gazed at him with her eyes closing.

"Eddie . . ."

"Did you hear about Marla Samuels? How she almost got herself killed?"

"What now?"

"Grinding feed for their poultry, she got her skirts mixed up with the belts. When she tried to get them loose, the machine threw her into the motor. She struck a big iron kettle when she fell. If her daughter hadn't been there with her, who knows? She broke five of her ribs, and that husband of hers hasn't left her alone since."

Kyle squirmed and I set him to my breast, imagining it—Marla was a mousy woman, the whole lot of the Samuels seemed shrunken and skittish and far too easy to please. Eddie cleared our dishes and stood for a time, watching us. "He's a good boy."

"He is."

"Doesn't take much after Jack, now, does he?"

I looked at her and Enidina gave a quick nod and turned her back to me, washing the tea from our cups. "All this waiting," she started. "It teaches you something." Her voice was low, her hands working, and I knew she was talking about what Jack had sent me for, though Enidina would never admit she was telling it to me. "Patience," she said, as if reminding herself. "When it comes right down to it, I suppose it doesn't matter where a child comes from or why. I suppose it never does."

I shifted Kyle uneasily, and he began to doze as he fed. The air in the room was heavy and dull and soon the sound of water in the sink set me to dreaming—I shut my eyes. Enidina gripped my shoulder and I let her hand stay, though the weight of it was painful in its grief. As Kyle slipped from me in my weariness, she took him up and settled him against my chest. When at last I woke, I was alone in the dark kitchen, Enidina hovering somewhere in the house behind me. Kyle rested in my lap and I heard Frank come in, his singing from the other room echoing like a hymn—I listened, not knowing what made this house so easy and full, no matter how poor it seemed, and why I always came to it, why it was so different from my own.

When the days grew dark again, I made my way to the chapel, freeing the piano from under its heavy cloth—I had not played since Kyle was born, had not attended services since I was well and pregnant. Now I sat on the piano bench with an ear to the room behind me, Kyle asleep in the basket at my feet. Trees whined against the windowpanes, the wind heavy over the fields, but inside the air was hushed. I struck the keys—the room echoed, and I struck again, making little that could be called music. Kyle stirred without a cry, without even a whimper, as if he knew my reasons. Borden stayed in his rooms, head in his sermons I guessed, and at last my fingers tired. I rested my hands in my lap, my chin to my chest. I had not prayed for a long while, fearing God himself might have turned his back on me—now no matter how I called Him, that lifted-up feeling in my chest never came. What an empty place, this cold, pitiless room without even a voice to listen to, without a hand to take—when I ran my fingers over the keys again, it seemed I hit every note at once.

Borden opened his door and I stopped my playing and listened. The day was bright, the sun through the windows lit the room with stains, reddening my music on the stand. At the back of the chapel, Borden stood with his legs wide, his shoulders hunched, as if braced against something. "Are you finished?" he said.

I did not answer, my eyes turned to my lap.

"I said are you finished?"

I shook my head, my hair loose against my shoulders and neck, and my skin seemed to stand at attention. I pressed my hand into the seat next to me, expectant, but when I looked for him, I heard only the door to his room fall shut—the light through the windows shook, the red on that page falling to my stomach. On the floor at my feet, Kyle opened his eyes.

In the months after I brought Kyle to the church, I could not sleep more than an hour without waking, could not be bothered to eat but a few bites from my plate. I stood on the rug in our front parlor with a broom in hand and forgot what I had wanted with it. My own husband was lost to me, gone it seemed for weeks to the fields and the weather. I tried to keep up with my chores, bleaching our linens and washing grease from our plates, the front of our shirts, but the work seemed different, cheerless—the mere ironing of a sheet undid itself as soon as it was finished and had to be done again.

Inside our barn, I ground feed for our chickens, the belts stretching and pulling at the grain. Grinders were ill-tempered machines—it never took much for the motor to stick, throwing sparks. I shoveled in more grain, enough for the grinder to choke, and thought about Marla Samuels and her skirts—the way she had been thrown at such a speed and how hard she hit that kettle to break her ribs. What would it take? For months Borden had acted like a stranger to me, and my husband came in like a bear to my kitchen, that wildness in him hidden beneath a dark pelt. When Marla was finally well enough to walk, she held on to her husband's arm as she strolled through town, that bandage of hers high across her middle. The townspeople worried over her, endlessly, and her husband refused to drop her hand.

The smell of burning filled the barn, the grinder whining against the feed. The air was thick with dust, and the motor spat and pitched, my eyes watering from the smoke. Bending closer to the noise, I imagined myself caught, my skirts like feathers and the floor trembling with the force when I was thrown—what would it take? I gripped the fabric of my dress, thought about the break of bone and muscle, how quickly that pain might diminish if a wife was determined enough, if she could feel the heat of a man's hand against her cheek—and in this town, she would be treated like a queen. The grinder was less than inch from my hip, the wind of its belts tickling the hairs on my arm.

Beneath the roar of the motor, I heard a small voice. I blinked against the light from the open door—there was my youngest. He bit the tip of his finger, stumbling forward on his newfound feet. How he had grown, his eyes black and sharp, his hair dark and skimming his shoulders—the way he stood seemed more like a boy than any infant. How many months had it been?

Kyle wobbled and fell to his knees and I swept him up, out of the barn, and coughed in the open air while the motor burned. Outside, Jack had heard the noise and come running, but now he stopped and watched me as I stepped out of the smoke. Seeing the way I clutched Kyle to my chest, Jack bit his cheek, and everything that had been cold and dark in my husband seemed to break. I had done it. I had skinned the beast and left him naked, for surely Jack knew what had happened with the Samuels and what I intended— the way a simple chore could prove itself worse. He touched Kyle's head as it rested against my chest, his fingertips rough, catching strands of the boy's hair where they stood from the back of his neck. The grinder squealed and Jack's shoulders twitched, but my husband stayed holding on to Kyle just where he was.

VII

Enidina

(*Spring–Fall 1920*)

After I lost the second one, I was bedridden for a time. It wasn't that I was too tired to work or too pained to lift my legs. Something in me wasn't right. Some sadness I couldn't undo. The women in town did their best to show me how wrong I was to pay so much attention to what I'd lost. I guess in a way I knew I should listen.

They came every day for a while, bringing books and new linens, a change of clothes. As if I had none of these in my house. I thought of my brother's wives and how little I knew of them. How little they cared to know of me. These women weren't much different. They seemed bound by duty, sharp in their ways. I must have appeared peculiar to them. I didn't gather in the shops to talk. Didn't find the reason. When once I baked a pie for the church sale, they threw it out believing it burnt. I had a husband but no children, and that made me odder still. "Get up, this is no way," they said. I couldn't tell one voice from the next, only that what they said was true.

It was Frank who had taken up my dress to wash it and Frank who had thrown out the plates and cleaned the floor. When I woke to find him missing from the room, I sat up in our bed. "We sent him off," the women explained, lifting a gown from around my shoulders and putting on another one. Their faces changed from one day to the next. It took me days to understand they were different women altogether. Members of the church, wives of the men who owned businesses in town. The farm women nearest couldn't have spared the time. Save for Mary. But I never saw her once.

When Minister Borden came, the women left us alone in my room. He stood over the bed, his fingers pressed together like a tent. The quiet in him seemed a relief from the women and all their rush. When he drew up a chair, I realized how the years had tired him. The cuffs of his shirt were yellowed and worn, his chin dark with stubble, and he had a cut on his cheek. He smelled of soap and polished wood and looked as pale as a ghost. "Eddie," he started. The last time I'd seen him, it was weeks before Kyle was born. I'd found Borden in the church kneeling in front of the pews. He pressed his forehead to his knees, his hands clenched over the crown of his head. His knees on the floor looked pained, bony as they were in loose flannel pants, and he made no sound, only a labored sort of breathing. The kind when grief takes hold of a person and shakes him through. He's just a man, I thought. At a loss like the rest of us. I couldn't bring myself to comfort him, private as his grief was. Now at my bedside, he sat with his eyes closed, and I remembered how I'd left him to himself. How sorry I felt for doing so. That day in the church, I doubt he even knew I was there.

"Have you ever lost a child?" I asked.

Borden blinked. "No," he said at last. "But I do believe there's meaning in what happens to us. There's a reason."

"You think?"

"There are times . . . ," he said, but left off. "After we came here, I asked my father the same thing. We had almost finished the church by then, but my father was restless. Looking back I should have seen he wasn't well. He was sitting in his chair where we stayed then in the back rooms and he folded his newspaper to see me. 'God makes mistakes,' he said. He didn't bother to explain. He just sat there with the paper in his lap, not reading. I've always thought of that when something happens. 'God makes mistakes.' It's little comfort, I know, but it's a reason. My father died a few months later. I have no other family. Not compared with yours at least. I'm afraid I'm useless in that."

"No one?"

He shook his head.

"Must be hard off alone. Out there, I mean."

Borden took out his Bible, as if he was through with talking. The pages were tattered and he clung to them eagerly, reading to me in a quiet voice. It was a story I didn't know, but there was a rhythm to it. His voice brought some comfort. I thought of him in that church without his father, nothing but air between him and that ceiling. How do you comfort a man who speaks to spirits? He seemed more of a child to me now than anyone and I tried to keep myself awake and listen.

Finally Frank was with me again and the rest were gone. He squeezed a towel over the washstand and washed my arms and legs. Soaking the towel again, he let the water

spill from his hands. He washed my cheeks then, my throat
and chest, and I swallowed under his touch. When he was
finished, he wrung that towel out well and laid it on the
stand to dry.

Next to our bed, a handful of daisies stood in a jar. The
blanket under my chin smelled fresh, and my dress hung
on the closet door. How Frank must have scrubbed it, for it
was thin and almost no color now. But it was clean. It was
respectable at least. Still, I would never wear it again. Not
even for him.

I'd been thirty the day I met him, late in a woman's life for
marrying. Even now I remember the afternoon in all its heat.
I'd started out to my eldest brother's to spend the night,
more than five miles by foot, and stopped in town along
the way to get a drink of water. In the country store was
a young man, tall and very thin, the look in his eyes as soft
as cotton. He was there to visit cousins, or so he said. The
merchant introduced him as he would any stranger in town.

He was just old-fashioned enough to shake hands. I nodded and drank my water. The men went about their business. But every time I looked up, I found this stranger's
gaze on me. I didn't know if it was because of my roughness or the red of my hair, the heaviness I carried. I'd never
drawn much attention from a man before. Nothing that was
kind.

Finally he asked, "How is walking?"

I was timid and backward then. No better now I suppose.
With the water on my tongue, I kept my mouth shut.

"Speechless," he laughed. "Well now, I never would have thought. Still, a person only has so many words in him. A person has to be careful. Otherwise, he might just run out by the time he's old, and there's no helping a man who can't speak his mind. I know for myself this is the most I've said in a very long while and I'm just about spent." He clutched his throat, pretended a look of pain. "I've seen it happen. My uncle, his jaw hanging but not a word, and nobody knew what to do with him. They said when he was young he was always just yammering on . . ." He scratched at his ear and grinned, blood rising to his cheeks. I just about spit that water out. He reached out his hand, wiped a drop from my chin. It was then I learned his name. Frank, he said.

My boy, you may think it girlish, but that's what I'd always believed my husband's name would be. Frank. A name that promised someone good and decent. Someone who might not mind a woman who said her piece when she thought it useful and otherwise said little at all. A man honest more than proud. At the time, I thought this Frank might be him.

You must understand what a shock it was for my family, their aging daughter, as strong as any of the boys and without a delicate bone to speak of. Frank brought me to my eldest brother's in his wagon, and my brother wondered at him in silence as he took us into the house. We sat together in the kitchen, the table bare between us. All of us were worn with travel or work. The evening had grown to dusk. Upstairs, my brother's wife paced the hall. After greetings on the porch, she had left us alone. The kitchen itself was quiet, save for a loose window that rattled in its sill. Finally, my brother spoke. "Frank," he said, "you ever drive a four-horse team?"

"Since I could tug a rope," Frank said.

My brother clapped his hand on the table and looked outside. "Well then, it's too late in the day for travel. It's not even day any more." His wife's footsteps had stopped and he leaned in to speak to us. "We've got a cot out back. Would you be needing a place to sleep?"

"I would," Frank answered.

"Well, there you are then," my brother said. "It's yours."

I don't remember much of that night once I closed my door to sleep. I've never been one for dreaming. Never seen the use of it. But I knew a man slept near me in my brother's house and that seemed important. Early the next morning, I woke to help my brother with the milking, and there was Frank. He waited out back in the yard, fixing a hat on his head to join us.

We walked out in the darkness and didn't speak. Mornings like that have a quiet a person doesn't want to break. There's something precious in it, precious too in how close to sleep it seems. The light when it comes shows the richness of the soil under your feet. The cows are close with the scent of milk, their eyes dark and lush. We brought them in from the outdoor pens and lined them up, keeping our tongues except to whistle at the animals when needed. After steadying a cow in its catch, we straddled our stools and pulled the buckets between our legs. Frank worked as well as my brother did, though he didn't know which of the cows had a temper or were slow to milk. He sat with his hat low on his head, his hands in an easy rhythm. He worked those cows as if he'd known them his whole life.

I probably did the same. I've always had a way with animals, or so others have said. It's sympathy, I guess. I take what I need. No more. No less. I treat them as creatures that know pain and stillness and the pleasure of a stomach when it's full. Just the same as us. That morning at my brother's place, I drew up my skirts to fit the bucket between my knees and pressed my forehead against the animal's flank. I could feel her breathing, knew she was nervous by the way her ribs shuddered. Those cows smelled good and warm, the smell of hay and something sharp enough it makes your eyes water. Some might call it a stink, but that smell has always been home to me. It's the same as the smell of my skirts after a good day's work, the heat of my lap. As I milked, I talked to the animal hushed-like. Nonsense it was, but calming. My brother did the same. Then I heard it. Someone was humming. I'd worked in barns most of my life and never known such a sound.

I turned my head and saw Frank. He pressed close to his cow, straining his neck so he could see me where he sat. He hummed as he worked, and the cow chewed at her hay without a twitch. That humming was low and clear. A song I didn't know, but familiar all the same. Not calling attention to itself and quiet, barely more than whispering. That's when, you see. You might not understand how your grandmother would go with a man who was little more than a stranger. You might think it was handy for us or that our families wished it. But really, it was the way that sound filled a dark place and stayed with me for weeks. Even now I can hear it. A kind of brightness. And Frank, he seemed to think a woman with such a soft touch on an animal was worth watching. A woman who'd never lost a bucket, who didn't mind the itch of a cow's hide against her cheek. He seemed to think that was something. And I suppose it was.

It was later that morning after breakfast that Frank shook my brother's hand and brought me home in his wagon. The air was cooler that day as we went. It promised rain. When we turned onto the road where I'd always lived, it looked like a foreign place. The gravel beneath us lay rutted with wet. The grasses were a strange silvery green. This was the beginning, I thought. This shrinking of all I'd known, it promised a new life. The trees stirred and I stretched my limbs. The ground beneath our wagon leveled off. We stopped just far enough from the house so Frank could tie the horses, and there was my mother. She must have heard the jolt of the wagon wheels, for she stood in the yard out front, squinting under her hand.

"Mother," I called. "This is Frank."

"Well, now. Look at that," she said. She studied him as he fed the horses. "Just wait for your father," she said and turned back to the house. When she came out again, she held two glasses of lemonade. She pressed one into Frank's open hand and stayed to watch him drink it. After that, she brought him a second glass and hurried us to the porch where my father waited.

"Let him be," he started before my mother got another

word out. "Eddie isn't the kind to sit in the kitchen and be still," he said to Frank. He had already grown ill, my father, though we didn't know it. He'd aged a great deal in the last few months, heavier in his steps and late to rise, the hair at his temples white. My mother often found him asleep in his chair. She had to call his name more than once to wake him. My father had lived in this house since the day he was born, my mother joining him when she was seventeen. Now they had four grandchildren, two more on the way. With Frank next to me, I couldn't think they'd ever been strangers to each other. "Eddie has a hand in everything on this farm," my father went on. "She can heft the grain and birth a calf, lead a plow with the best of them." Hat in his hands, Frank listened with the new glass of lemonade empty at his feet. "She's a different kind of girl," my father said. "She won't be spending a lot of time in front of the mirror with curlers and what not."

Frank scratched his ear after my father finished and seemed to stew awhile. Through the screen, our grandfather clock chimed the hour. The sun fell behind the clouds. My mother and father looked at him, expectant. "That's just fine," Frank said at last. "That's all the better." He opened his hands and shrugged. It was then I saw that easy way in him that made marrying and all the rest as simple as closing your eyes when you grew tired or eating when you felt the hunger for it. "I must say I'm partial to her," he added. My parents had to lean in to hear him.

My boy, you may not believe it, but the second time I thought I found you in town, I remembered my Frank the way he'd been that morning in the barn. There you were, trailing after some woman, and she kept reaching back to take your hand. You would give it to her for a moment, but slowly let your hand slip. You would have been eight then. This boy must have been close to the age himself. *Mountains!* your mother wrote in another of her letters, from Colorado this time. *So high a person gets headaches walking the streets. There are plains too, but they're nothing like home. Too dry for growing much.* November fifteenth. I have marked the day your mother was due on my calendar for years. When you turned seven, I went so far as to fix you pancakes for your birthday dinner, just as your mother liked. I used plenty of butter in the pan so the edges would crisp. I kept them in the oven, piled on a warm plate. Waiting for you, I must have fallen asleep in our sofa chair. When I woke, it was early morning and the sweet smell had turned sickly. I opened the oven and the edges of the cakes were dry as boards, the middles a soggy white. Still, I thought those middles must be worth saving and I ate them myself. Fifteen cakes as wide around as the reach of my pinky and thumb. I've never liked food to go to waste, but those cakes put me in a bad way for a week.

But birthdays aren't what I wanted to write about. At least not yet. When I saw that boy in town, I thought he could be you. You, if only he'd been longer in the legs and narrower in the mouth. Breaking from the woman's hand, he scrambled after a dog in the street. He never knew it, but he ran right past me, pressed close as I was to the side of the old meeting hall. When the dog got away, the boy stopped close enough for me to hear him humming. It wasn't even a tune. No melody I could follow at least. But there he was, breathing hard through his nose to get the notes, making them up as he went. For a moment, I was back in my brother's barn. I was with Frank, with his slow gaze and his easiness, the way nothing seemed to rumple him or take that grin off his face. And I believed that I might be more than imagining. That the boy I saw before me might just be you. But when I looked again, he was gone.

I spent many a rag cleaning the floor of that kitchen once I was out of bed. I could never quite trust it. For months, Frank worried about my taking on heavier work, and the days turned long and terrible. When once he found me nodding off with a pair of his good trousers over my knees, needle in hand, he took me by the arm. There was a revival, he said. Outside under a large open tent, no less. He knew I didn't care for sermons. Too much chatter. But he believed there would be a great many people gathered there, enough maybe for me to forget myself for a while.

In the morning we set off on foot. Frank talked as we went, taking my hand if I fell behind. He said when the ministers grew hoarse, the musicians would bring out their instruments. Then, Frank said, how the people would sing. It would be good to hear after what I'd just lost. At the time, I saw no more children to come. We traveled the gravel road for miles and crossed fields. In the sun, my hand sweated in his. Stepping out across the tracks, Frank came at last to a stop, though we hadn't yet reached it. "Look Eddie," he said, his arms drawn out. "Look over there." And there it was.

The tent was taller than this house and covered most of a field. Around it were smaller tents, the color of burlap. The canvas was brown with dirt and heavy with rain from the night before, the grass gone to muddy footprints. The tents stirred in the low wind, the ropes straining to hold them. People stood by the hundreds inside.

We slipped through a gap at the back of the larger tent and others made room for us. They were strangers, most of them. Folks who'd traveled more miles than we had walked. Borden stood in front, hands above his head. When he saw us, he broke from his sermon as if surprised. Borden wasn't the long-winded kind. He didn't belong with the red-faced men and their starched collars who sat in a long row behind him, waiting their turn. When he started again, I can't say I listened. I was too tired to stand for much. "He'll be done soon," Frank said. "Look at him. He's already running out of steam." I wanted them to sing.

It was then I saw Mary. She stood at the front with her new boy in her arms. Her skirt hung loose from her waist and seemed to have lost a stitch, her hair pinned so the skin at her temples stretched. I hadn't seen her for months, not since she'd come to our house with Kyle. After only an hour, she had fallen asleep in my kitchen and I couldn't do anything but watch. That's how tired she was of mothering. That's how tired we all were, I suppose. I'd held her boy's thumb as her head nodded and dropped. I didn't think once of letting go. When finally she stirred, I left her to wake as she would. I didn't want to hurry her. I still had the milky scent of that boy's thumb in my hand, one I could keep with me for weeks. I thought then that

Mary and I might become more than neighbors. That we might be friendly for once.

Now Mary turned and saw us. She dropped her chin against her boy's head and breathed in. Borden kept on. "What are you saved from?" he was saying. "Are you saved from pride? Are you saved from longing?" Around us, men and women clapped their thighs and called out to each other when they agreed. When they had committed some terrible sin or hadn't done a thing and still they felt ashamed. I held my tongue. The woman beside me kept her hymnal closed around her middle finger. Others used ribbon or scrap to mark a favorite page, but soon all of them had opened their books. At last, the noise of their restlessness made Borden stumble, dropping his hands. You would know it then. The people were ready. They were ready even before the music began.

That's when I heard it, the like of which I hadn't known since I'd stood by Mother's piano when I was young and listened to her at the keys. Since I'd watched my brothers sing with their guitars. There were guitars here too and horns, even fiddles. The women tilted their heads to reach the higher notes. The men sang into their chests. No one stayed still but rocked on their feet, and the children played in the dirt beneath us. I could hear Frank then, the way he always sang, but more. The sound of him warm and deep. It was a song I knew. Something ordinary for churches and plainer places. Something good and plain and loud. I sang low as was my voice and it was easy, this singing. This wasn't preachers telling us what to do. It was something inside us, rising. It opened inside my chest, a tremor to wake my sleepy head.

My boy, I hope you are never in as dark a place as mine was then. But with that singing, I imagined enough wind to lift the tent. If we could have seen it again from the road or from farther down the field, what a wonder it would have been. The hundreds of us. The quiet of the field wrested from it. We had made it. As Frank had promised. We had come just for this. What a noise we put out.

VIII

Mary
(*Spring 1923–Fall 1925*)

"I've spoken of sin before," Borden began. "But when you think of sin, I believe most of you see it as something you can touch. You can point to it, smell it, sense it. It is something you can find evidence for in the physical world. But I tell you, sin is much more difficult to grasp." The congregation stirred, feeling Borden's finger on them—I crossed my legs on the piano bench. I had expected the church to be half empty, but after the fire outside town, the chapel seemed to rise out of the fields like a beacon, and a line of carriages stood in the yard. There was something in this man now that caught our attention—with the dark of his eyes and the pallor of his cheeks, his hands seemed to hold all of us in his grip.

"As the Proverbs tell us," he went on, "the very thought of folly is an offense. *The very thought.* Sin is something far more than we can touch. For God, to even think of a sinful act is the same as having done it." A woman stood from her pew and sat weakly again—a few of the men dropped their mouths to their fists and grudged against something deep in their throats. My hands felt thin and limp where they rested in my lap. Borden went on, but I saw only his fingers as they struck the air, and the opening and closing of his lips. When finally he had finished, he closed his book, and those hands in my lap seemed as frail as paper. In their pew, Jack and my eldest sons sat tanned by their hours in the fields, as if they had carried the earth and stink of our farm in with them, while Kyle remained pale between them—but it was Jack who signaled to me with the drop of his chin. I took a breath.

Clumsy at first I played what I could, though the surfaces of the keys were slick to the touch. The piano droned, the strings struck dully in their case—where were all those years when I had balanced that board on my knees? With the thud of my fingertips and my mother's humming, how brilliant I had sounded then. Borden stood at his pulpit, gripping the wood. He had never been a man who showed himself well, staying closed off as he did behind his robes and the walls of his room. I felt for him, as I often had, for his strangeness in this place, his loneliness, and all that he kept hidden.

A slow thing happened then—a man cleared his throat behind me and I knew the sound, that low guttural rumbling, as well as I knew the shape of the bones in my wrists. My husband was watching me, like a furnace I felt him, and as I stretched my arms they became fine and delicate again, almost weightless. I closed my eyes and my hands grew swift, all of my husband's wildness rising out of me. How clear and light it seemed, the sound under my fingertips quivering into the room. It turned and echoed, keeping them all at attention. With Borden holding on to the pulpit and the heat of my husband at my back, I had never before felt so grand. I played on, moving from one hymn to the next, never breaking. Behind me, the congregation shifted in their pews—but I did not want to finish, not yet. I was not ready to give up this new place I had found, a place where I never had to choose and had done nothing wrong. At last, the groaning of the wooden seats grated against my every note, and with a final chord, I lifted my hands.

The chapel was quiet save for the piano as it hummed. The air stood on end, the congregation in their seats. Borden raised an arm to begin the prayer, but no one lifted a finger to their books. When I turned my head, Jack clapped his hands until the noise echoed in the hall. He was the only one. He stood in the pew and brought our sons to their feet, and in their fear of him they clapped as well as they could. Jack never did seem bothered by what was appropriate, and the congregation stared at him as if at a defiant child. But he was that large of a man, he could do what he wanted, and what he wanted was this—to be the one who made a fuss because he thought it was right, he thought his wife deserved it, and he wanted everyone to know that this wife was his. The others rose to their feet with the look of animals herded in their pens. Jack stood with his back straight, nothing like the beast who had kept himself hidden for so long. Here was my husband, the same man I had found outside the store with that terrible voice ringing out. I choose him, I thought— after all these years, after three sons and my fingers wearied from the work—I choose him, and I would, again and again.

It was the height of summer later that year when my husband gripped my shoulders where I worked in the garden and told me to sit.

"What for?" I asked.

"Not telling."

"But it's dirt here. I'm just about covered, and you know this seed won't hold another week . . ."

He put a finger to my lips. "Stand then," he answered, and from his pocket he took a bright handkerchief and covered my eyes, tying a knot at the back of my head. "For being the most difficult woman I've ever met, that's what for," and when he closed his hand over mine, it pinched. "Don't you look. I warn you." He led me up the steps to our house, so quickly I almost fell, and stood me in the doorway to our parlor—in that room, I heard a boy laugh out loud and then another, boys I knew.

Jack undid the knot behind my ears. "Look."

My eldest sons pressed close together with Kyle caught between them, a blanket raised behind their heads and the end draping the floor. They dropped the blanket with a flourish and only then did I know why they were laughing— in our living room stood a piano, one of my very own. It was a solid oak upright, newly polished, with pink ribbons tied around the legs and a large bow on top.

"What's this?" I gasped.

My sons ran to the instrument and tore open the lid, banging at the keys. The ribbons fell and tore under their feet, and they pushed at one another on the piano bench.

"Boys," I called out.

"This is for you," Jack said. He said it so loudly the boys stopped as if struck and slipped from the bench, trying to set the ribbons right. Jack put his arm around my shoulder and pressed his lips to my ear. "This is to keep you home," he said.

. . .

Over the next few months, I practiced every afternoon until I almost forgot there was planting to do and bread to bake. But no matter how often I played, I could not return to that feeling I had found in the chapel. Outside, the spring became summer and summer turned to fall, the rain bringing the cold again—for a week now it had driven so hard I could barely hear the notes under my hands. When someone knocked on our door, I stopped my playing and listened—the knock came again.

"Eddie?"

Enidina stood on our steps, spitting rain. When I reached for her arm, she stayed as heavy on that step as a stone.

"I heard you play," she said. "I forgot about that. Is it all right?"

I looked her over—such a strange way she stood, crouching beneath the weather with her red hair dark and slicked back from her forehead, her skirt heavy against her thighs. She kept her arms bound about her waist, moving like a ship. All those years with my walks across their fields, she had rarely come to our own. "Such a house," she said, stepping in. "I'm always surprised by how big it is." But it was not the house that worried her—it was something she had carried in with her, her hands cupped against her stomach as if nestling a sick bird.

In the parlor, I motioned her to a chair, but she sat herself at my piano bench. "I never learned to play," she said, her eyes on the keyboard. "My mother did." When she touched the keys, the sound stung.

"Your mother?"

"She wanted to teach me. But milking makes your fingers rough. I didn't have the hands for it."

"You had a piano growing up?"

She stood from the bench without a word and walked to the other end of the room, scooping up a small piece of knitting on the table and dropping it at once.

"Jack got me that piano," I said. "Next time you hear me at church . . ."

"Next time?"

"I'll sound like Brahms. That's why Jack got me the piano. For practice."

But Enidina was no longer listening. She had circled back around, wandering the room like a child, fingering doilies and bits of paper, her cheeks heated and her hands rubbing at her spine. I thought of her slogging all that way through the weather—she had not worn a coat, not even a hat to keep the wet from her eyes. "Mary," she said at last. "I felt something." She slumped on my bench again and spread her fingers over her stomach. "Sometimes you wish for something so hard you think it's true, and maybe I'm just wishing. Maybe I didn't feel anything at all."

She looked up at me then, her eyes shining. "There," she said, pressing her stomach. "I felt it in the house and came over as fast as I could." She bit her lip, but I knew she would never ask anything from me outright.

I stood next to her and reached out my hand, her fingers parting from her waist as she drew in her chin. Her stomach felt heavy and thick, the dress she wore too rough, but underneath, her skin was taut as a balloon. When I pressed my palm down, her breath rushed and I could smell the rain on her. Underneath, her heart beat through her skin and the skin jumped, the hard bone of a child's elbow or knee in its womb—there it was. Enidina sat on that bench like a queen. She seemed as large as a house, as large as the weather coming down—she took up everything.

"Eddie," I said.

Enidina sank back in a sweat. I should have known with the way she came into this house, as if walking on glass.

"Sometimes you wish," she said.

"For heaven's sakes, Eddie. This isn't your first time. How long has it been?"

She sagged on that bench as if sleepy, though her face held a powerful light.

"This is more than wishing," I said. "You shouldn't be out in such weather. Not in your condition. You know you never should." I thought of the rain from all those years before and the afternoon I had sat alone with Frank as he slept—he was little more than a stranger and there I was, miles of mud and wind our only company. Back then, I believed if I touched his skin it might have already grown cold, and then I would carry that coldness home with me, I would bring it into the very rooms where I cooked our food and laid our sheets, and even my husband's heat could never undo such a touch. "Be careful," I said to her, if only to fill the silence, but as I said it, I knew I wanted it to be true—what would she become if she lost another child?

Enidina shivered, her clothes soaked through to the skin. When I tried to speak to her, she took to her feet. "It's good of you," she said and swayed where she stood, her stomach in her hands. The front of her skirt was stained with wet, different from the rain, and a puddle ran from between her legs.

It was hours before Jack and the boys would return from the auction house in the next county, and now I realized that Frank must have gone with them—that was why Enidina was alone in her house and why she had come to our own. There was no one else for miles. She fell against the bench again and rocked in a daze. I tried to lift her, but she was far too heavy, and we slid to the floor. "Eddie?" I said, shaking her. "You've got to help me. At least try."

"Mama?" My youngest stood at the top of the stairwell, rubbing sleep from his eyes, the hair wild on his head.

"Stay upstairs, do you hear, Kyle?"

But already he was running down the steps, his bare feet slapping the wood. When he reached the parlor, he clung to the door and stared.

"She's having trouble, Kyle. That's all. Nothing to worry about."

Tugging at the corner of his mouth, Kyle padded to my side and rested his hand on my arm, but when Enidina groaned, he jumped. "I'm going to need your help, Kyle. I have to get her upstairs and I want you to run to the kitchen. Fill a bowl of water from the pump. Be sure it's clean and get some clean cloths. Stand on a chair if you have to. It's all right."

He scampered down the hall, and I eased Enidina up until she was sitting. "Come now, Eddie. Can't you stand?" She sweated and heaved as she lifted herself up.

"I should get on home," she whispered. "I can do fine. It won't be for a while." But I was not so sure about that, leaning on me as she did while I took her up the stairs. I marveled at my son, clattering about in the kitchen beneath us and the weight of that bowl as he carried it up. I put Enidina in bed and she smiled at me before wincing again. When Kyle came in, his eyes were wide, his arms straining, but he carried that bowl better than I would have expected—he did so without complaint or question, just as I had asked.

Enidina cried out and I lifted her higher on the pillows behind her back. Kyle set the bowl at my side and stood on his toes to see. "Take that other cloth and wipe her forehead with it," I said. "We need to keep her cool, just like I do when you're sick."

Kyle pressed the cloth to her forehead and Enidina opened her eyes. His hand brushed her hair and he hushed her like I often did with him, singing at the back of his throat as if trying to sing her to sleep. Enidina quieted. "Well aren't you a sweet boy?" she said. "Aren't you the one?"

"Don't look now," I told him and lifted her skirts to wash her legs—Enidina cringed at the touch. When I pulled the cloth away, it was heavy with blood.

"I don't want to lose this one, Mary," she said under her breath, her eyes to the ceiling.

"Kyle," I started, trying to keep my voice steady, and the boy came to my side. "I want you to do something. Something you've done before, but not alone. Do you think you can?"

Kyle gazed at me in his sleepiness, his shirt twisted around his belly and arms. I pulled him out of the room.

"Get your shoes and coat and run to town," I whispered to him. "As fast as you can. Don't stop for anyone, you hear? When you reach the market, I want you to ask for Dr. Stephens and they'll take you to him. He's got to come fast." I pushed the boy down the hall, squeezing his shoulder before he went. He slid across the floor, his arms raised from his sides as if trying to keep balance. Leaning against the wall and sick to my stomach, I pressed my nails into the soft underside of my hand until my dizziness was gone.

"I like that one," Enidina said when I came back, the air in the room already sour. "He can stay here if he wants. He doesn't have to keep out."

"Kyle's not like his brothers," I offered. "Not at all."

"No," she said. The front door opened and shut and I listened for my son's footsteps in the yard. The rain had ended—it would be light for another hour or more and warm enough. It was quiet then and we stayed together, Enidina breathing and me willing Kyle down the road as fast as I could without trouble, without so much as a scab on his knee should he fall.

"Kyle was always different," I said after a time. I thought about this room I had laid her in, how I had birthed my oldest boys in this same bed, with only the coarse hand of my husband for comfort and a midwife at the end—I never would have imagined so much blood. In little more than a month, those boys clutched my skin so fiercely that I could only think, *let go.*

"I waited too long," Enidina said under her breath. "I should have come right over. It was hours ago, just when I woke. I thought I was imagining."

"Don't you worry about that now," I answered. Down the road, I believed I could hear my youngest scraping his feet over the mud, his heart beating beneath his shirt. When I was pregnant with him, I dreamt such terrible dreams. Walking to his crib in my sleep, I would pull back the blankets, and there was no child but only a part of one, squirming on its back without arms or legs or a head to let it cry, but cry it did all the same—I could hear it again now, that same muffled wailing, and I imagined him fallen in a ditch or worse.

"Thank you," Enidina said.

"For what?"

"For trying. Even if I lose it."

"None of that. I've known women who've had it worse. For myself, I thought I'd lose every one, and I only had Jack."

"Three of them," Enidina said. "I don't know how you did it."

"You keep them living, that's all. And when you get to sleep, you're so tired you can't even think." Enidina had seen only the birth of animals—from the sickened look on her face, I knew it—the nights in the barn with only the light of a lantern, and the hot smell of the cow bellowing, men rolling up their sleeves in case they needed to pull the calf out.

"I can't imagine even one," she said.

"You will."

"All I'm saying . . ."

"Listen, there's no use talking like that."

"All the same."

I told her how fast my oldest boys had grown and how wild they were, how I used to watch them play in our yard, a stick in hand, always beating at the ground. The day my eldest turned nine, they left a rabbit close to dead on the front porch and asked if I could cure or cook it—as if they never knew the difference. I pressed the rabbit against my chest and pushed my fingers into the fur—such a soft thing, and just above its belly, its heart beat like a bird's. My sons stared up at me with a look of wonder, and the rabbit's eyes blackened as I held it close. From the day Kyle was born, I knew he was different from my eldest two, but Kyle was the one I had to send off. Watch it, I would say. Be gentle. I coaxed his brothers to stroke a cow's hide as if it were silk, but their fingers gnarled the fur, and there they went, running off like bandits through the fields while the poor beast was stricken with knots, too nervous to let a small hand touch its side again.

Enidina closed her eyes and a contraction ran through her, her hands on her hips as if trying to hold it back. Over the fields the wind pitched and fell, and I squinted to hear any other sound.

"You did your best," Enidina said at last. I hushed her and stood. Not far down the road, gravel scattered and a heavy motor ground its way toward the house. The sound came again, louder this time, and the motor stopped. I ran to the window and looked out—in the growing darkness, my son was not even shivering as he walked up the drive, looking taller than his five years and somehow having lost the stumble in his legs. He pulled the doctor by the arm, the man in a dark coat with his head down beneath the weather, drops of rain spilling from his wide-brimmed hat. The downpour had started again through the mist, the doctor's car smoking like some hot-blooded creature behind them. With his chin high and his face streaming with wet, my son walked along as if he had birthed Enidina's child himself, as if he had washed and swaddled it and already named the child his own, and when he opened the door of our house, he led the doctor up the stairs and down the hall to us, all the while telling the man how she was.

I did not see Enidina again for weeks, not until they let her come home for good. Twins, they said—such was her luck. They were small and weak and stayed with the doctor for longer than any mother should bear. Enidina sat with Frank in the back row of the church, holding on to herself. Her cheeks were doughy and full, her mouth showed hints of a smile, but in her eyes was an inward look that said she was trying not to think of anything at all—not of how she could lose them, not of how something might still go wrong. She sat in the church and held her own, wishing the time would soon pass for any such thinking to be possible.

"Best stay home after this," I told her.

Enidina relaxed into her seat, and that inwardness in her eyes lifted. "I'll stay home when I'm ready," she said, without a hint of bitterness. She took my hand and squeezed it in both her own until my knuckles cracked.

In the months to come, I would see her holding her new boy and girl in that back pew, one in each arm. They had Frank's black hair, but otherwise looked as different as their own parents—the girl thin and fair-skinned like her father and the boy a meaty bundle with Enidina's powerful limbs. Who would have known Enidina could be a mother to so much? She held on to those twins as if keeping the world upright, and when they grew to stand and fret at her feet, her hands kept them close. There was something in Enidina's strength and stubbornness, in her very size—with her tight hold on those children, she alone seemed to be holding off the terrible events that were to come to us.

This was the day of my youngest's baptism and the first Sunday we did not trek off to the lake to have it done. At the front of the chapel hung a velvet curtain with a small room behind it and a pool waist deep, as wide as three bathtubs. Jack and I stood in the front pew with Kyle between us while Borden read the prayers. Jack had worn a suit for the occasion, his only one. He tugged at the throat and stood his full height, nodding along with Borden's words as if they meant something to him—maybe they did. For such a man, I knew words had never carried much weight. If anything, that was the difference between them—Borden with his books, and Jack fighting to count, to speak, stumbling until he used a fist instead.

When the time came, Jack gripped Kyle's shoulder and steered him out of the pew, but Borden met him in the aisle face-to-face. This was the first the two men had stood so close. Behind us, a woman in the balcony sang a low, awful hymn. Two other boys waited in their robes at the edge of the pool, their hands folded at their waists. Borden took Kyle's hand, but Jack kept hold of the boy's shoulder, and my son twisted between them, looking from one man to the next, neither giving in. The woman lingered on the last note, the song ending in a dying hum. Finally Jack let go.

"We are here together to welcome these boys into our congregation," Borden began. He dropped a robe over Kyle's head and it gathered on the floor. "Washed from the sin of their birth," Borden went on, "these boys will soon be ready for God to receive them." I closed my eyes and took Jack's hand—his grip was hard and he held his arm straight so I had to bend my knees to reach him. "Jack," I whispered, but already Kyle was wading down the steps to join Borden in the pool, the boy's robe rising in the water as if to swallow him. Borden reached an arm around the boy's shoulders, Jack twitched, and I wished that terrible woman would sing again. At last Borden drew him back and the boy went limp. The water rose over Kyle's face, and the pool grew still, Kyle disappearing under Borden's robes for too long a time. Something deep grumbled in Jack's chest and he twitched again. Borden shook himself as if caught in a dream and pulled Kyle up at once, but the boy was gasping, water running from his shoulders, his hair—he seemed about drowned.

"He shouldn't have done that," Jack whispered. Borden rested his palm on the boy's head as if to settle him, but he seemed nearly drowned himself, his hands shaking. Like cousins, the two looked, or more—cold and pale, their hair wet, and Kyle with those black eyes of his, filling. Jack tore his hand from mine and bounded to the pool, taking the steps two at a time. "You shouldn't have done that, Borden," he yelled.

Borden stood out of the water as if he had been hit. "You can't—"

"You're the one who can't," Jack said. He shoved Borden back and hoisted Kyle from the water, tucking the boy under his arm. When Jack faced front again, he looked out at the pews. The sun from the southeast windows made him squint, and he must have seen what Borden had every Sunday for years—that line of faces, silently watching as if they had come for something special, when Jack must have thought there was nothing special about it, just a boy nearly drowned and work to do at home, the day already late for beginning. Dozens of men rested back in the hard wooden seats as if they had never been farmers, could not even hear their own animals bleating in the barns a few miles away. How did they have time for sitting? Then Jack was running. He pushed past me where I stood in the aisle and rushed between the pews, the doors swinging after he left.

I raised my head. The others strained to see the back of the church where Jack had gone and crowded the aisle. When they heard my heels on the floor, they turned to let me pass, watching for what I might do next. "A shame," a woman said. Though no one spoke a word more, I heard them all saying it, one after another, and I followed my husband out through the double doors. Those good years, I should never have trusted them—that violence in Jack, it was always waiting. I should never have thought my playing for him that day in the church had lessened it, or any of the days since. I stood on the chapel steps and Jack was running far off down the path with the boy in his arms. He stopped and set Kyle on his feet and rushed on, leaving the boy behind. I called Kyle's name, but he was running along himself now, trying to keep up with Jack no matter what the man had done. All the way home Kyle would do that, but Jack never did wait, not for either of us.

IX

Enidina
(*Fall 1925–Spring 1933*)

Those twins had been my first. The first that lived. I remember how Kyle had come in after the doctor and the way his mother tried to keep him out. After they were born, that boy stood watch while I slept with a newborn under each arm. When both the twins fussed, he touched a finger to their lips and looked as if he might cry himself. How strange they must have seemed to him, red and small and still smelling of the bed with everything I'd pushed out. He was just a little thing himself, with the boyish scent of sweat and spit. But ever since, Kyle watched over my own as well as any mother might.

I should have known they were coming. In the months before, I'd taken a liking to the feel of dirt on my tongue. With my first child, the dirt had tasted of metal and snow. With the second it was almost sweet, filled with leaves and twigs. Before the twins, the earth seemed grainy, like bread. I'd heard of such cravings in women. No one looked on them kindly. But out in the fields, already covered with the stuff, tasting the earth I sweated over seemed right. A kind of nesting. Borden had said we were made of so much, after all.

After the twins were born, I was uneasy with them and seldom left them alone for long. Frank said I should be sure of them, these sudden children. But I didn't know what had been right in me to bear them out. I found some old gunnysacks that seemed good and sturdy and fitted them so I might have a hole for my head and a seat for the twins to kick their legs. Outside while I worked, one child hung to my front and the other to my back. "The Hunchback," Frank called us, grinning. "The Terrible Three." I waved him off. This place and what we'd raised on it, it was suddenly my own. I felt a comfort from their weight. A steady strength. As long as I carried them both, the twins never fussed.

I'd never known what it was like to have a part of you looking back. That birthing meant you carried that child with you for the rest of your life. As they slept, I held my hand above their mouths to feel the warmth of their living. Their need of me, I was embarrassed by it. Never before had I been the object of such attention, as if I deserved it simply by bearing them out. Maybe I did. My boy, I don't know how any woman makes sense of what she's carrying, before or after a birth. It took me a while myself to understand.

It was before the twins were born, before I even knew I was expecting, that Jack raised his barn. From our yard, I heard him drive the nails and split the wood. It would take a year and more of careful work, as Mary wouldn't let their boys help him much. Holding the twins in my arms, I watched Jack build it after they were born. Over the fields the frame of that barn stood in the distance, and one at a time the walls went up and stayed. Jack finished the roof of that barn, painted the sides a dark red. Those twins of mine grew. They dropped from my hold on them and learned to walk, learned to speak their minds and carry out their chores better than any mother could expect. But what Jack did. Nothing seemed so great in front of it, so terrible, as the red on that barn from so far away.

The years after he finished it were the worst years we'd seen. The price of farm products went to nothing. A bushel of wheat cost a dollar to harvest, but sold for less than half. Corn was ten cents, hogs three dollars a hundredweight. Barely a third of what we got more than ten years back. We burned grain for heat in the winters. It was cheaper than coal. When the banks closed, they raised the interest on our mortgages and most of the farmers couldn't pay. Just imagine it. A man works a piece of land all his life. Then he loses it. It is stolen away from him. So desperate did some of them become, they decided to take things in their own hands. Up north, the farmers blocked highways, wouldn't let a neighbor from the next town pass for trading. They dumped his cream in the ditches, his butter and eggs. They wanted to force the market, keep the produce from moving. On the railroad, they burned a truss bridge to stop the freight. I couldn't imagine taking up such violence. It seemed as much against the government as against our own kind. But I knew the way they felt, cornered into saving themselves like that. They didn't find such actions easy. I knew that too. All of us, we lived good safe lives. We watched over our own. We didn't ask for much except to be left to ourselves. And we weren't the only ones.

This was the time the tramps appeared on our roads. They wore burlap on their feet. Carried a pack of clothes and keepsakes, if they carried that much. They were from the south and west, most of them, states where the droughts had struck. They looked for work, and if they couldn't get it, begged for food and water. Sometimes a barn for sleeping. In the mud in front of our house, they marked our path with a circle and a cross, so small a carving that I didn't see it for months. Still, I understood what it meant. Ours was a safe house. We would open our door. Give them what we could from our pantry. In those years, we were never that far from needing the same ourselves.

"They're covered in dust in the west," the tramps told us. "Black blizzards. There's a long dry spell coming." The way they said it made us lean in to listen. They cradled their arms against the rain as if they carried a child, as later they would carry our food.

Frank listened without a word. He seemed to be listening even after the men were gone.

"They had mud on their feet, Frank," I reminded him. "Didn't you see? There's so much mud here they can't walk in the ditches. Dry spells, they're saying, but they keep to the middle of the road."

"There's women with them now."

"Well, so, there's women."

Frank looked down the road to where one of the men sat, hunched over and chewing a bit of our bread. Sitting on the ground, the man had soaked his pants through, but he didn't seem to know it or care. He turned his head to the sky and tore at the bread with his teeth.

"Something else bothers me," Frank said at last. "That new agriculture man in Washington. Secretary Wallace.

He's got the government ready to buy and slaughter all the young pigs and sows set to farrow."

"At the end of the season?"

"Wallace came too late. Couldn't get the bill signed before the pigs got pregnant, but he wanted it through anyway. Jack says it'll raise prices. A lowering of production, he says. And it's legal this time. None of that mischief like we heard of up north. They'll even send the extra meat to the people who're hungry for it."

"Legal doesn't make it right."

"No," Frank answered. "And the way I hear it they don't have enough men to process what all they've got. The packinghouses can't handle the smaller pigs, so they turn them to grease, if they use them at all. There's not enough places to store the meat, either. So now there's people starving and it's rotting somewhere. Down in St. Louis, I heard they threw thousands of those pigs in the Missouri River. But the local association, they still want us to sell. They say anyone who doesn't would be taking advantage, getting the raised prices off the backs of the ones who sacrifice now. And Jack, he's all for what the association wants."

"Since when?"

"Since he needed the money, I guess. Of course, that's not what Jack says. He says he doesn't want to be a traitor. Against the government, maybe, but not against his own. 'It's done,' he told me. Like I didn't have a choice."

Frank grew quiet and I took a step back, thinking about this killing. A knife across their throats and the young ones not yet grown. That was the terrible thing. Those newborns didn't have an ounce of meat on them. And they wanted the sows too, just because they were pregnant. It would ruin us. The kitchen empty. Frank forever thin. No sounds from the barn except its settling and the rot of what we'd taken too soon.

"I'll not have you do it."

"No," he let out. I stood listening for more from him but none came. Such a wonder, the way this man could move in and out from me. But in this he was certain. "How are you going to keep them?" I asked, but I didn't care much about the way he did it. He would figure out something. That husband of mine, he was a fine smart man. I'd known it all along. Now when he set off for the barn, I followed.

The rain of that fall closed us off from the outdoors. It kept us in the house, sleepy in the low light and bound to the stories we told. We heard more about the drought in other states. That summer we had been more than dry ourselves. But the rain had come again with a vengeance and it hadn't stopped. Donny and Adaline, our two dark-haired children, marveled at everything. Why the rain came. When it would end. Why the floors of our house were damp, and what we kept inside the barn. We took pleasure in telling them the time of day when they asked, showed them how to count their numbers and spell out their names. We explained hot and cold, good and bad, with all the lines children want in between. In our stories we described a place we saw fit to live in, an order of things we felt to be right. Being alone, being far out in the countryside, we created the world as we wanted it, and we made ourselves the makers of everything.

I have pictures of the twins in those years, from the time they were born until they turned eleven. In one of the last, Adaline has a hand over her brother's shoulders. Even as a child, your mother had a prettiness about her, with her father's black hair and thinness but my own almond-colored eyes. She kept enough of me, at least, to give her some weight in front of that camera. Looking off into the darkness, Donny stands next to her as if he grew out of his sister's skirts. He was the bigger of the two, sun-blackened and sturdy, but beneath Adaline's arm, he folds himself square against his sister's ribs. Like a proud old dog he looks, keeping to his owner's side.

Since they were born, I'd brought the twins with me to call the cows in from pasture late in the afternoons, just in time for the evening milking. A month before the rains came, I heard them on the back porch getting ready alone. When I looked for them out the window, they had already headed off, a good twenty-minute walk. Cows may seem dull and slow, but they are powerful creatures. They can rush a person if they get fidgety, and back then, the twins stood only as high as the animals' flanks. Now in early spring, it would be dark before the cows might come back home. But the twins knew the path by heart. Since fall, they'd been walking it themselves to school more than two miles out, the pasture a shortcut that led to the county road. I went along this time in case they had trouble but followed far enough behind so I couldn't be seen. It wasn't unusual for a farm child to take on such work. But like me and my own brothers, I knew they wanted to do it alone.

Adaline and Donny walked side by side down the scarred path, leveled by the cows' passing. The light had dimmed, that colored, sideways kind of sun. The air smelled of metal from an early rain. When finally they could see the pasture, the twins sang at the cows from a distance. The herd crowded together by the slough where they drank the last of the snowmelt, bumping flanks. The twins came at them with their hands over their heads, their shoulders high, making themselves bigger. They circled wide around the herd on either side and drew together at the back. The cows stirred, turning their heads. They tore a last few bites of grass and then moved all at once, the lead in front, loping along. Every once in a while one of the animals startled. There would be a rush. But behind the herd the twins called out, as small as the youngest calves themselves, and the cows slowed.

I went back to the house to start dinner. Adaline and Donny would haul wood for me when they returned. They would gather peas and tomatoes in buckets from the garden and go to the well to clean them and bring them back. It was a while I was waiting for them. Finally, the two came striding in. They already had the wood in their arms and a dozen or so corncobs to keep the fire going.

"I've been expecting you," I said.

"We got the wood ourselves," Adaline answered.

"Adaline wanted to," Donny said, and he grabbed a bucket for the vegetables. Adaline jerked her head at him and he grabbed her a bucket as well.

"Looks like you're doing plenty yourselves."

"Sure," Donny answered. "We're almost done."

Adaline gave him a cross-eyed look. "Almost," she said.

They went out together then, buckets clanging. Beyond the kitchen window, they crouched in the garden, digging through the dirt. They set the tomatoes in one bucket so as not to bruise them, the peas in another. When they set off to the well, Donny carried both buckets by himself. Only eight years old and those two already seemed grown. But no matter how far they went, they would be all right. As long as one had the other, I believed they always would.

During those weeks of rain, Adaline and Donny grew closer still. They walked the miles to school together with tin pails for their sandwiches and came back early to finish their chores. Being so far out, they were often alone with each other, though at times Kyle joined a half-mile along. Even after he'd finished his eighth year, Kyle went, though he hurried home soon after to help his father. There were only twelve children in that schoolhouse, most far younger and living closer in, so those three grew as dear as cousins.

The hogs stayed in the barn and the weather let them sleep. In this keeping of them, we never doubted ourselves. When we heard the animals stirring, we fed them early and well and kept all that was important in our world as close as we were able. It was a powerful time and we believed a bit in what was coming. The drought to the south and west and the trouble it would bring. But it was hard to be certain of anything outside our own hundred and eighty acres of land.

Where he sat with us on our porch, Frank would sing, his voice deeper than I'd heard from him. *Bring me a little water, Sylvie*, he sang. *Bring me a little water now.*

Adaline puckered, blowing a curl from her eyes. Donny cocked his head and frowned. They sat at our feet, drawing a picture between them with a piece of charcoal. In only days it would wash off.

"That's right," I said. "Your father's asking for trouble. That Sylvie has already come."

Frank sat forward in his chair, singing, and Adaline slapped his arm.

"Aren't you the smart one?" he laughed. He bent down and lifted them heavily to his knees. When Adaline dropped her head against Frank's shoulder, Donny did the same. *Getting mighty thirsty, Sylvie*, he sang louder. *Getting mighty thirsty now.*

Small rivers broke the soil, the grass gone to mud. The sky hovered over us as if we should kneel under what it sent down. We were safe under that porch, wrapped in blankets and drifting, near to sleep as Frank grew quiet. Under our breath, we prayed for the rain to hold off or to stop altogether, watching for what would come.

I suppose a person should never wish for things too hard. Something bad often turns up. Sometimes when I squint at that nurse, I think Adaline is home. I can smell the same cream on her skin, like blackberries. The way she tilts her head on her thin neck. My boy, in the last few months I've found myself wishing for your mother so often I feared I would lose myself to it. Now Adaline is almost here again, looking sharper than herself and a bit like someone else. When the nurse brings those buckets for my bath, I try to behave as any mother might.

"That's it," the nurse says. "I always knew we could get along."

I turn over for her. "I've made a wreck of it," I say, but the nurse doesn't seem to hear. The water is prickly against my back and I think I might choke. She squeezes the sponge and claps her hands when she's finished. I wonder if she'll ever tell me who she is. She's nearly my age, I think, with her white hair pinned back, her square black shoes. But she's much too thin, too quick on her feet. With me in this bed, there must be more than twenty years between us. When she dusts Kyle's picture, she presses her face so close her breath fogs the glass.

"That's my daughter there," I say, reaching for the bureau. The nurse picks up the photograph behind Kyle's, and Adaline peers out, all curly hair and drive.

"She writes me," I say. "Sometimes she does."

"You know where she is?"

"Not for months, now."

"But she writes."

"Now and then."

The nurse looks away. "You must have an address," she says. "When you write back?"

I lift the bed skirt, though it leaves me panting. Underneath are all your mother's letters in a box, the ones she's sent in envelopes and the others I've tried to write myself. Some are only half finished. I got tired of writing pages I couldn't send. The nurse sorts through the box, studying the envelopes before throwing them aside. With her face so close, something about her flickers in my head, but just as soon goes out. "That girl, she's the mother to my only grandchild."

The nurse pauses.

"Donny," I say and close my eyes. I feel the nurse watching me and she goes back to rustling through the box. The light turns. The front door creaks on its hinges. When I open my eyes again, the nurse is gone and I know I've been asleep for some time. In the dimness I can smell those blackberries, but the smell drifts. The box is under the bed, this notebook covered in dust. The photographs are back as they were, with Kyle in front. Sometimes I wonder if anyone has been here at all.

We were sitting on that porch when we first saw Jack on our road, and we knew he'd come to see us about our hogs. His hat was low on his head, spilling rain to his lips. His jacket blew from his sides as if it ran along with him. Frank sat forward in his chair, knuckles folded under his chin. "It's him," he said. The children grew quiet, even Jack's youngest. Back then, that boy often escaped his father's house and stayed at our own. I never minded keeping Kyle from Jack's hand, not with the way he watched over the twins. Now with Jack like a stranger rising out of the weather, I hurried the children inside.

Jack took the porch steps in a single stride and threw himself into the chair I'd left. "How're the boys?" I asked from behind the screen door. "How's Mary?"

He took off his hat and shook it, his face pinched. The children played at the table behind me, spilling soup. Kyle shouted a dare to the twins, and they tried to drink their bowls in one swallow, losing most of it down their fronts. If not for our neighbor's presence, I might have joined them. But Jack was stewing, scratching his thumb against a knot of wood on the porch rail.

"That's enough, Kyle," I called out.

"Do I have to ask?" Jack started. "You haven't done it, have you? You've got to change your mind. Go in with all of us."

"I don't see why," Frank said.

"We've already agreed, that's why. It wouldn't be right if one of us held out. Nobody will have his hands clean when this is done. And if you don't come along, you'll just ruin it for the rest of us. Make us all look bad, and you so high and mighty."

I laughed. "You haven't done your own yet, have you? That's what I expect."

Jack turned to me behind the screen, his face hard.

"What is it, Jack? You want to be sure they're no holdouts so you can stand it better? Here you are, pretending it means nothing. But I bet you think it means plenty."

Jack looked at me and blinked. I'd hit home, but his face covered up quick.

"You know what they did to that judge up north, Frank?" he started again. "The one who got so happy foreclosing farms? They shook a rope at him. They dragged him out of that chair in his courtroom and tarred and feathered him. Left him like that in the town square. And what they did, they did it together. Some people thought it was crazy, but it took planning. It made things happen. Now Roosevelt is listening. The president is. Not like Hoover. He only made shacks. But Roosevelt is trying to help. It's what they've been fighting for, and it's good money they pay, almost five dollars a head."

"You're the only one here that cares about that money," Frank said. "That five dollars is for seventy-five percent of the herd. Only seventy-five. And it wouldn't matter if it were a hundred. It's a waste and you know it. You work and all you make is used. Not a bit thrown away because there's no extra from nowhere. It's who you are." Frank took a hard wipe at his chin. "Once they're gone, there's no going back. It'll ruin the farm selling them like that. They're not even grown."

Jack wasn't looking at him. With his head down, his hat closed off most of his face. "This isn't something you can sit around and think about, Frank." Jack took to his feet and swept past me at the door. "Your mother wants you home," he shouted, pulling Kyle from the table.

"Don't you dare," I started at him. "That boy hasn't done anything."

But Jack had already pushed past me again, knocking me against the wall. He was out the door then and the boy had to run to keep from being dragged. Still, Kyle did his best to keep up, almost as if he had wanted his father to fetch him. As if he craved any kind of attention from the man. The two went off together across the yard and Jack yelled back to Frank, loud as if he wanted the house, the road leading in, and the whole countryside to hear him. "You do it, Frank."

In the days that followed, Frank crossed to the barn and back again, carrying slop. He kept a good watch over the hogs, his shoes muddy and stuck with chaff, his shirt wet, clinging to his ribs. He was slow to step into the house, covered as he was with the barn stink. My fingers grew strong with washing and his overalls ribboned. I patched them with burlap and thread.

Days and nights of this and we never could rid him of the smell of those animals. He stood in the rain and let it run from him, keeping an eye out for anyone on the road. If Jack wanted to raise a fuss, he could have sent the association to pay a visit. Every man in the association could have come on his own. But we didn't hear a word. Only the tramps came, carrying their bread now under the front of their shirts. That mark they'd left on our path had long washed off, but I found the same circle and cross carved on our tree out front. To them, we were still good folks.

When Jack came again, it was a meeting Frank was ready for. I could tell he hadn't slept with thinking about it, the way he bowed his head when he saw that man on our road.

"Where are they?" Jack yelled before he'd quite reached us. "I just wanted to be sure. I didn't want you to do anything stupid."

Frank crossed the yard to meet him, the toe of his boot knocking Jack's own. "I'm keeping them," Frank said.

"No, you're not."

"In the barn." Frank looked at the barn, his head cocked as if listening to it. The sun broke through and Frank turned his face up and squinted, his mouth open. Weeks of rain it had been. So constant we felt drenched to our bones, our teeth swimming. Like wood, we'd swollen inside our clothes. And there it was, the bald and drying heat.

Jack was past him then, knocking Frank on the shoulder as he headed for the barn. This was what he'd meant to do from the beginning. Frank had challenged him to it. His steps were no different from the way he had walked up our road, his stare low and his hand tight against his leg. He drew out a knife and I rushed off the porch to follow him, calling out to Frank.

But Jack was quicker than me. He saw us coming. When he ducked into the barn, the hogs squealed and I knew he was at the little ones. Inside, the light was full of chaff and scurry. The horses threw their weight against the stall doors, their heads twisted to see the back wall. Jack crouched in the shadows, sweat-soaked and rising out of the pen. "Eddie," he said, as if he'd never expected I might be the one to stop him. He held one of the babies squirming in his hands, red-faced as he was and trembling. So full of fury he didn't seem to know what he wanted to do or how. I believed he'd always been that way, clenched against that tireless blood in him. He closed his eyes and cut into the animal, cutting his own fingers, and he threw the animal down. Then he was off again, his face streaming and a low howl in the back of his throat, ducking through the pen to get at another one. I grabbed him as he chased and he fell under me, cutting my arms with his knife. Behind us Frank yelled and the air cracked with gunshot.

Jack stiffened and let go. For a moment I believed Frank had done it. He'd shot the man. Sitting up, I held my arms close and bleeding. Jack lay on his back, his eyes swollen and red, but there wasn't a wound on him. The fight had left him empty, and he lifted his head to see us both.

"I'm keeping them, Jack," Frank shouted. He was breathing hard. The shotgun was heavy in his arms but he kept it aimed, ready to fire.

"No you're not," Jack let out. His voice was little more than a whisper now. "Not any more."

Frank could hear the pigs before he opened the pen. He saw the dead one first and the rest, nine babies, cut up and whining. At the far end, the sow ran untouched, flies humming at her flanks. With his mouth set, Frank gave me the gun and grabbed Jack's knife. One by one, Frank took up the babies and cut their throats to quiet them. The sow ran in circles against the wall, mad with grief and worry. Her quickness had saved her, but her shoulder was still bloody from bashing the wood, the gate shivering and about to crack as she hit it.

Frank crouched in the dirt and swept his hands over his face, watching the sow. She was tiring and soon lay down. Jack slapped his hat against his knee and groaned, the rain coming off him. Frank caught him by the throat. "If you tell anybody about that sow," he said.

"What?"

Frank pointed Jack's knife at him. "Don't tempt me. It doesn't make a difference. Pigs or Morrows. It's all a waste and it's killing for no reason."

Jack hit at him and Frank let go. "What does it matter now?" Jack said. He was on his feet, wiping at his eyes and shaking. "I did what you couldn't," he said. "And you'll always owe me for it. You best hurry now and take those pigs to town before they rot."

X

Mary
(*Spring 1933*)

He was my husband, but I never thought I would see a man in such a fury, and see him with all that was good and constant drained out of him, and doubt him for that, be scared of him for that, and it was never his choosing, but what the government decided that led him to it, that made me love him less.

"It's done," he said when he returned from the Currents' farm. He held his hands at his sides, palms open, as if repentant.

"What's done?" I asked.

"We're ready now," he said. "We can go ahead with our own." He wiped his mouth against his sleeve, and I could not imagine what he had done, his coat ruined and such a stink. "God help you," I said, taking his hands, but he wrenched them away. For days then, Jack's eyes were red-rimmed and brimming, never letting go of how ready he had said he was, how much it would take out of him to finish it, but he did not touch those hogs of ours for weeks, for no better reason than he never could bring himself to waste so much.

He would kill the hogs with a club—that was the first idea that burned through him, beating down on something. He never thought of a quick way of doing it. He never thought of knives, not now. Blades were for meat, but this was just killing—"Got to remember that," he said, as if making it harder on himself, making it feel more like work, could somehow give that money we got more meaning in the end. He tested the strength of the club in his fist, and I saw how he would strike with it, and how I would lose him to it. The club's weight took his whole being, his back, his shoulders, splinters in his hands.

I went out to the Currents' farm myself to see what it was all about. No matter how ugly the thing Jack might have done, what we had to do would be worse. Enidina was carrying empty feed buckets from their barn, but when she saw me on the road, she stopped and the buckets clanged against her thighs. She studied me, chewing the corner of her lip, but at last she nodded and invited me in.

"Terrible," I said to her, sitting in her kitchen.

"Yes." She nodded and tried to smile, her fingertips drumming the table between us. "It's good to see you, Mary," she offered after a time, though she seemed strained to say it. "I worried we might not, after all." She swung out her arm as if to indicate the room, though the house was empty of anyone but us. Remorse, I thought—it was making her quiet, though something in her eyes hummed. "What with Kyle coming here before. With the trouble he's got, and you being neighbors. It would be a shame, that's all."

I cleared my throat. Trouble, she talked about, but Kyle had no trouble, not the kind a mother could not take care of. "I wouldn't want you to think we hold a grudge," I started and settled in my chair. This is a woman I have known for years, I reminded myself, a woman who gave birth in my own house, who ran through the rain and chose our door to knock on, scared and shivering and sick of herself—Kyle was not the one with trouble if he could help a woman like that. "Jack wouldn't want you to think it either. You were just slow, that's all."

Her fingers stopped. Fine red gashes crossed her forearms and I wondered about them. She saw me looking and sniffed, not bothering to cover the gashes with her sleeves. "Jack hasn't done his own, has he?"

"It's a sacrifice," I said. "But it's a sacrifice we all have to make."

"That man, he couldn't do it knowing ours were alive. And he pretends to be so hard. All his noble reasons. You should have seen him when he left."

"That's what neighbors are for, for helping. That's why he came here in the first place. Doing for a person what a person can't."

"Help?" she said. Enidina's fingers struck the table again, as if I was telling her something new. "And see here I thought you might be coming to say you were sorry."

"Jack's upset about what happened," I offered. "You know the way he gets." I thought about those arms of hers still, ten or more gashes altogether and each of them as straight and thin as a blade. "I can only think there must be something I can tell him to calm him down, some words of thanks on your part, that might set things right."

Enidina sniffed again and stood. "You should talk to Jack about that," she said, and she said it with the same look on her face I had seen from her years before in her field, studying me like a stranger without so much as a glass of water to cool my throat. "I suppose Jack's mad about something and it wasn't any of our doing. I believe he's been mad about something on that farm of yours for a long while." That look of hers, how long ago was it?—when I was so tired from walking and could feel the cut of every stone under my shoes, and I almost lay down in that field as she worked, I almost did, that woman on her knees and wiping her hands while I closed my eyes to rest.

"Enidina," I said, though her name caught in my throat. Jack had been mad a long while before this. I was just about to explain again, get her to understand how easy it would be to ask for forgiveness, but already she held the door open to let me out—as if Jack and I were the ones to do her wrong. I sat for several minutes ignoring her, and at last the door fell shut.

"Suit yourself," she said. "I'm not one for forcing. Not here we aren't," and she left me for her chores. Outside in the wet air, the twins ran from their work in the barn, covered in chaff and dung and looking little better than orphans, dressed as they were in patched denim and cotton undershirts, even the girl. They were good-sized children, already eight by then, but each could squat in the crook of one of their mother's elbows, wrapping their arms around her neck. Enidina marched out into the fields like that, a large, lumbering beast with her brood, letting the mist cling to them as if it was no different than sunshine. As I watched Enidina go, that house of hers seemed full of wind, the door still banging and not another living soul to tighten the window screens—not even Frank. When I returned home, Jack was squatting in the dirt outside and kneading that club between his hands.

The local man had said the packers had more meat than they knew what to do with, and keeping the meat ourselves would only turn the others against us. "Slaughter the pigs yourselves and bury them," he said. "It's your only choice now."

I stood over the sink at my kitchen window, watching my sons and their father make their way out to the barn. They looked like fierce gray animals, my husband marching through the mud and my sons running after him. The older boys, they were men now—large and plodding, almost indistinguishable from the young Jack as I had known him, though they lacked his warmth. They had stayed at the farm during those early Depression years, when there was nothing else to leave for, though by now they both should have had wives and farms of their own. Now all four of them crouched together as they went through the rain—Jack in a rage knowing he had waited too long. The barn was theirs, a place for men, as certainly as I had my own room in our house, where I could keep some semblance of tidiness and right-minded living, while the barn darkened and grew, as virile as the animals inside. But as I watched them go, I knew I would have to follow them, however much Jack would not like it. If it was happening, I would need to witness it, just as God would witness it, so I could fix it in my mind and understand it and know where best to lay the blame.

I stole out to the cover of the barn, hidden by the rush of the rain. My sons stood outside with their father and beat the hogs in turns, Kyle holding the animals so they would not struggle too much or slip away, so it would not take too long—but no matter how he held them, his brothers beat down and missed, for the little ones refused to be still. The club rushed close to Kyle's face, stirring the hair on his head, his father's hand bloody with splinters. With that club, Jack never bothered to look at what he hit, the animal or the ground.

They would bury the hogs in different places around the farm so none of us could remember where they were or re-member doing it at all. The government man had driven in and closed the check in my husband's hand. "It's a good thing," the man had said. He wore a tan suit, thinning at the elbows, and his paunch strained his belt, the little hair left on his head oiled and combed, but his face was young, not a line in it. "For all of us."

"Good," Jack echoed.

The man wiped the sweat from his neck—a boy's face, I thought, but the man smelled nothing like a boy, not even when he turned to me and smiled. "Sorry to interrupt your dinner," he said. He put on his hat with a long look, and his hand left its print on our glass doorknob. At the win-dow, Jack crushed the check in his fist and watched the government car slide onto the road. The car alone made the man different.

"It's enough," Jack whispered when I asked how much the check was.

"For what?"

He dropped his chin, the check falling to the floor. "We could have taken in boarders, but you said no," he started, clearing the table, the plates small in his hands and the silverware smaller still. He seemed to weigh them in his fingers. "We could have had one or two. That might've made a difference."

"And make your wife a servant?"

Jack looked at me, and those plates and silver flew, a fork clipping my ear. He fell into his chair and dropped his forehead hard against the window, gazing at the road, but outside the man was gone. "It's enough," I whispered, cupping my mouth. Bits of egg and grease clung to my hair. "It's plenty now." A different kind of life, I thought, but not with that man and his car—I could not even imagine it. I was done with thinking of other lives for myself.

"Look what you made me do," Jack said under his breath. "Nothing to feel sorry about." I lowered my head—this was the man I married, the stone on my finger and the heavy band. I had made my choice. Still, those gashes on Eddie's arms troubled me as did the rest of it, like a fly buzzing in my ear, a furred and ugly insect, too quick to catch and get a good look. Knives, that was what Jack had said he used on their hogs. Now where he sat, Jack seemed to shrink into himself—how little strength he really had, too little when he needed it. Finally he rose from his chair and kicked it from under him and walked out the back door. After I was sure he was gone, I found that check in a ball under the table and ironed it flat.

With that rain falling against the barn, my boys bent close together and never looked up—a father and three sons. Their boots were the color of mud, their hands, their shoulders, their shirts hanging loose. The sow was the last one. They had kept her after they finished the others because she was stout and pregnant, she would be easier to hold— because after they buried her, they knew they could never be who they thought they should any more.

And their mother, what would I be then? Because it had taken such a long, hard while for me to make this a good place, a place where goodness could be done. Jack had such a fever in him now and did every time he looked at the wiry build of my youngest, but I had done what I could to set things straight—I had washed my hands from the dust and stink, worked to make the best of appearances, and tried to keep Kyle from running off down the road to save himself from his father's hand. Now this butchering was soaked so deeply in our soil I had to run out and see it, to witness it and carry the terrible waste it was in my breast, and I did not think God or anyone else would be able to look on us as a high-standing family ever again.

My husband held on to that club while my sons gripped the sow, and I wondered why she had to jump around so, why she never simply lay still and suffered it like the ground—suffered it like that, the way the ground never resists a person's trampling on it. The club beat down and broke her, my sons wrestling to keep hold. When finally she stopped her jumping, I could see how she was swollen in all the wrong places, and I tried to think there was nothing else in her, nothing any of us should feel sorry about.

They carried her through the storm and I followed, taking little care in hiding myself now—I was a shadow to them, if anything, almost invisible in the rain. The sow's stomach sagged between them and they fumbled and cursed, the ground loose under their feet. When finally they dropped her, Jack yelled that he would go back to get the shovel. Together my sons stood with the sow between them and watched their father stagger home, going slow, unable to get his footing. The rain hissed and grew, making rivers in the mud, and my sons squinted under their hats and tried to find their father through the storm.

But none of us could see him now. That was the way he went, walking off through the mud, the last I saw of the man I married, the man I knew—he would always be gone after that, a man of fog and temper, he would never come back, not for the six more years that I would live with him and scrub his shirts and cook his meals. Those Currents had trapped him. They had promised they would do what they should and sent him off to have to finish it, or so he said, coming home with stains so dark on his sleeves that I had to turn that shirt to rags. After he walked off in that rain, you could not say we were husband and wife—we were little more than strangers. Later when the body of that man went, his passing was quick, without a shiver, without absolution. After years of keeping to his own, I found him again in our bed, stiff and cold where I woke in the morning next to him, my hand clutched in his. He must have come in during the night, so quietly I never felt the mattress shift, but it was the rush of blood in my hand that woke me when he released it. Still nothing more than a stone sat inside my chest, because my husband had already disappeared from me years ago in that storm.

Now my oldest son cursed him. "He's not coming," he said. "He's not coming back." He kicked the ground, and the mud and rain flew as high as his head.

Kyle wiped his eyes. Together his brothers looked at him as if the boy was the worst thing their father ever did. "You can bury her, Kyle," the younger one said. "All by yourself. Dad would want you to, wouldn't he?" Kyle wondered at them, but his brothers had already turned back to the house, their shoulders bent under the rain, their hands reaching as if they wanted to catch hold of something and wring it out. In less than a year, both would leave our farm for good, without warning, without even pressing their lips to my cheek—going off to the cities where they could get away from mud and pigs.

My youngest spit into the rain and studied the sow at his feet, tapping her with his boot. I reached out my arm, but he flinched. The storm swept down, the mud rising with it. It came over the toes of our boots, tugging at our heels. It ran deeper than our ankles where we stood, the sow sinking under it and the mud rising enough to bury her, if only by inches. Kyle fell to his knees and started digging, crying

now and digging with his bare hands. There was no stopping him. He lunged and dug up to his shoulders, the hole
falling in and the weight of the dead sow shifting. All at
once, the water in the hole drained and took the sow with it,
covering her until only the pink nipples showed along her
belly. Kyle gathered mounds of mud against his chest and
threw it over her with a desperate heave. Finally, he swept
the mud flat with the palm of his hand and stood as if wild.

That rain, it was gaining on us. It fell and washed the
mud from beneath our feet, rushing out until we had no
choice but to crawl our way home—and for years that rain
never came back.

XI

Enidina
(*Spring–Summer 1936*)

————

The way I heard it told you have to burn it out of you. You have to be strict about it. Consistent. The doctor had given me only months as I had the consumption, and I took to keeping turpentine and grease on my chest. Around my neck I wore a shawl covered with the stuff. Later, when my breathing grew difficult, I spent my nights sleeping in the fields. The summer of '36 was hot and dry, almost as bad as '34. The stalks of corn broke at a touch, the leaves yellow and bitten through. The daytime passed without a wind, the corn falling, but I was bent on saving it, my hands brushed with dirt for luck. I could taste the turpentine every time I coughed.

It had been three years since I'd had much to do with our neighbors. Three since Jack had come with his knife. Though we were slow in using it, we kept the money we got for the hogs he'd killed. Frank never let out what that man did. He himself had been the one, Frank said, who'd finished them off. Not Jack. I kept my opinions to myself.

Of any of that family only Kyle walked the distance between our farms. Every other day he came, and my Donny trailed after him as if the way that Morrow boy spoke, the fear and hunger in him, were the very qualities he wanted for himself. They went hiding out in the fields on "missions." Took to the lake for fishing, though neither seemed able to hold a line. As Kyle grew older, I'm sure he shared with Donny a word or two about drink and girls. I doubted Kyle knew much about them himself. Still, those bruises on Kyle, they must have given him a great deal of mystery, at least for my son. Time and again, I took Kyle by the arm and made him sit in my kitchen where I could doctor to him.

"It doesn't hurt," Kyle shrugged. "Not any more." The boy looked starved and fragile as a hatchling. I made a poultice and held him still until it set. "Does your mother know?" I asked.

"It's not Dad's fault," Kyle said.

"It isn't?"

"He gets mad, is all."

"But Kyle . . ."

The boy looked away. "Where's Addie?" he asked. He winced when he tried to talk.

"Upstairs," I said.

I took hold of his chin, moving his head back and forth to see the cut on his lip. He strained against my hand, trying to look up, and I looked up with him. Adaline jumped from her bed above us and slammed her door. I clicked my tongue, but Kyle wouldn't take his eyes off that ceiling.

"She's a spitfire, that girl."

He nodded.

"Going to be a handful. For any man she marries, I mean."

Kyle looked at me and reddened. "Gotta go, Mrs. Current," he said. "Gotta find Donny." He backed out of the kitchen, skinny and pale and limping. My fingers were sticky with paste.

It had been Donny's idea to learn the horse. He'd heard from Kyle about the animal's speed. Said the boy had showed him with his hand how high he'd sit on its back, how well he'd ride it. But I'd seen them walk home after only the first try, Adaline, Donny, and their father to keep them in line. With dust on his skin and clothes, head to toe, Donny looked anything but pleased about the way it went.

"You should have been there, Mother," Adaline started.

"The horse reared," Frank said.

"When he was riding it?"

"No, not riding it. Not yet."

Donny hid his hands behind his back, but already I'd seen how raw they were.

"Donny had just taken hold of the rope when the horse reared, almost dragged him under. That's what happened to his hands." Frank slapped Donny's shoulder, forcing a grin. "You know, Donny. That rope is there to keep the horse down. On the ground, I mean. It's not for flying." Frank tried to laugh, but Adaline stood from her chair, her eyes wet. "Now there," Frank said to Adaline. "It'll be all right. He just has to be careful."

"Addie," I said.

Frank reached for her, but the girl rushed up the stairs. "Adaline," I called. Her bed creaked above our heads as if she'd thrown herself into it. Frank drew a nervous hand through his hair.

I nodded to Frank to ease him and brought out a can of lard to rub into Donny's skin. I knew no amount of mothering could calm that girl. Not for a while at least. Even as they came in, the three had watched me, the shawl I wore carrying such a stench. They had a way of cupping their noses, breathing through their mouths. All of them were afraid, you could see it. Donny and Adaline stepped away whenever I came near. They bothered me if I stayed outside for long. The sun was too hot, they complained, or too bright. As if the light and heat could set the shawl afire.

I held my son's hands in mine, small as they were and bleeding. The lard would cool his skin, but peroxide might keep him from infection. Donny was tough and broad even as a boy, a bear of a child with my own build and temperament. But baby fat still clung to his fingers. The doughy cheeks he'd been born with, they hadn't yet left him. He showed the same bruises now as our neighbor down the road, but from an entirely different animal.

That horse. I could imagine it well enough. Imagine the way Donny could walk under the animal's flank without even having to bend. "Enough now," I said to him, though I couldn't be sure the boy listened. "Your father says you have to be careful. It's a horse, but it's a wild one. Keep your sense." I imagined the horse kicking him. One strike could send my son to the ground and then the speed of its legs as it ran. Donny pulled away from me. I'd been holding his hands too tightly, what with his sore skin. He stood from the table, twisting out of my arms, and I opened my fingers and let go.

"Don't mind him," Frank said, and clapped his hands on

the table to be done with it. But I knew it wasn't done. It might never be. With such an animal, I knew that at least.

We'd had a hard few years after the rains, as had everyone. In the summer of '34 we planted crops as usual, but with the drought we didn't raise a bite. The stock were starving for feed and water. It was almost too hot to breathe. From the nineties in the shade, the temperature climbed above a hundred and ten and stayed for fifteen days. Frank dragged a mattress out to the back porch and took to sleeping there at night with the twins. In the middle of August, a breeze came through my bedroom window about midnight and it sprinkled rain. I ran to tell them, but Frank didn't trust the weather enough to move his mattress. Still, from that day on it felt close to livable again.

Nineteen thirty-five was a poor crop year just the same, but we did raise a little something. Still, our shade trees finished dying from the burn-up they got the year before. The bank raised the interest on our loan and we had to let eighty acres go, but agreeing to bankruptcy saved the rest. This was almost unheard of then, shameful as it seemed to most. We knew other farmers talked about it whenever they met in town. It was the same as accepting charity. Taking something that wasn't yours to begin with and not paying what was owed, from the government no less. But we didn't have five hundred men to keep the state from bothering us, as they did over in Cedar County when the governor tried to test milk. And our neighbors wouldn't crowd out buyers from an auction at any foreclosure. After the trouble with the hogs, after keeping our sow, we'd lost quite a bit of trust with the town. Bankruptcy, it was different than the money we'd gotten from Wallace. It paid for failure, or so they saw it. Helping only the ones who asked. With the hogs, we at least had to do something hard, something like work. With bankruptcy, we didn't raise a sweat. And we'd benefited well from it, keeping over half our land while the others turned up their noses at any kind of handout. Still they lost everything they had. For weeks, Frank and I struggled over the decision. The land was ours. It was who we were. Those acres, they were our very life together. Some twenty-odd years of marriage and work.

It was the next summer that my lungs started to fill. The doctor listened to the liquid in my chest and ordered me to bed. At night I made myself a pallet of wood and blankets and slept outside near the fields. This did me some good. There was a slight wind, the smell of the ground. I breathed it in, wrapped my shawl close. During those nights, Adaline brought a blanket for herself and laid it out at some distance to watch me sleep. I kept my eyes shut, though I was well awake. Only when she believed I wasn't listening would she talk. "I've decided on it, Mother," she said. "I'm going to marry Stan Wilson. He's skinny, but Dad says boys change plenty by the time they grow, and his folks live in town. That's what I like." She was quiet for a while and I heard her rustle in her blanket. The moon was high and bright. She could have seen the shawl around my chest without even squinting. "You've got to be careful," she said at last.

That rustling sound, she was biting her fingers like she did when she worried. In the last year of my sickness, she was often biting them, so much I thought I'd have to bandage her hands. "That awful thing you wear."

I raised my head, shrugged the shawl from my shoulders, and the rustling stopped. "What about Kyle?" I asked. Adaline didn't speak after that, but still she stayed. After a time, I turned as if falling asleep again, and she let out a breath. It was a safe time for her to be with me. At night, the fires in her head seemed to lessen.

"Kyle," she said at last. "He's something, I guess." And with your mother, I knew that something was a great deal more. It was bigger than she knew herself. She wouldn't let out another word, but I could tell she was thinking it over. By early morning when at last she slept, I carried her back inside the house.

Already a sense of cool was returning to me. On those mornings when I brought my girl to her bed, she was light and easy in my arms. My chest felt loose, my breathing full. I was less afraid it would run out. Just before I slept, I could hear the leaves shifting and the groans of the good earth I believed still waited beneath the topsoil. The stalks, I imagined, were tall, well grown. And with the shawl around me, I seldom coughed.

But in truth, the fields were no different. The leaves hung with grasshoppers. Dirt drifted under our doors and through the cracks between the windows. In the distance, the horizon wavered like smoke, and the wind never stopped its grazing. This place had become strange to me, or I to it. I'd lived in such countryside all my life. I never thought I could survive in a place that wasn't as flat and plain as a plate, where little was hidden. Now the absence that hung over the land seemed something I could touch. Frank and I took to sitting on the porch in the daytime, watching the sun take our crops as it would. Before us, the corn hummed with insects and brittle leaves. A terrible, hungry sound.

It was Adaline who next took a fever, though the doctor claimed it wasn't the same as mine. Donny walked the road to the Morrows alone. He was so set on that horse, he refused now even to have his father along. Still, without his sister, that boy seemed just about helpless. The rim of his hat broke, his lip showed a bloody crack. Adaline's loyalty was that fierce. "He's home," I told her when she woke from her sleep, hearing his footsteps in our yard.

"That animal isn't right, mother," she said, sitting up.

"Have you told him?"

"It's Kyle. He's the one who keeps Donny going." She closed her eyes before she finished and sank back, already in a sweat.

The horse was worse with Donny every time. It wouldn't be tamed. Even Frank was convinced of it. Donny walked up the porch steps, threw himself into the shade.

"You should think about quitting this," my husband said, waking in his chair. "No harm giving up what never gives you a chance."

But Donny said nothing. Every day Frank tried to keep the boy home by not going with him, sure the boy wouldn't go by himself. But Frank never could understand stubbornness, not even my own. Adaline fell asleep again and I tucked my shawl around her throat and chest. By the morning, she'd have thrown it off.

At last I walked to the Morrows' farm to see the animal myself, to see what it was capable of. I stood at the edge of their land and watched from a good distance. Kyle held the horse by a rope, and the animal circled the corral. It kicked when the rope stopped it short, running and jerking in circles until the length of the rope stopped it again. Only when Kyle gave it free rein did the horse show itself well. It was smooth and tight in its running, its hooves carving up the dirt. But even from where I stood, I could see how skinny the animal was. How this running didn't have much to do with strength but with something more desperate. With its ribs showing, the horse twisted its pale neck, its eyes rimmed with white. Kyle whipped at it to keep it going.

The boy himself looked like a stick figure beneath the sun. Tall but hardly grown. Five years older than Donny but seeming less. He was an unusual one too, not big like his father but slight in build and delicate. His face had been beautiful from the day he was born. Still, on that afternoon, his limbs carried a kind of meanness. He stood with a girl his age who was curly-haired and slim, pretty enough for distraction, and Kyle called out in awe of the animal, "Look at him." But the girl couldn't keep herself from looking. Kyle must have known it as she held on to his arm, breathing hard the way a sudden wind does a person. This wasn't an ordinary animal. This horse was a powerful thing.

Behind the Morrows' winter fences, I stood my watch. The knot of the shawl rose and fell against my throat. The horse got little affection. Not from its owner or anyone else. Turning the rope, Kyle kept on and kept on while the animal ran. Soon he forgot the girl altogether, watching only the horse. Watching it and wiping the sweat from underneath his hat. I could see it in the way he stared at the animal, grinning. He liked to watch the horse go. He liked to drive it too far, just as his own father drove him, and every time the rope caught it short, I flinched. That horse was meant to go. It was meant to be gone.

That was the way your mother went. She had her reasons, what with you so unexpected and this place like tinder to her. My boy, before you were born, I'd seen how she grew with you, though she tried to hide it as much as she could. I knew it in the way she touched her hand to her stomach, stopping when she walked into a room. She caught her breath, the blood high in her cheeks. Under her hand was the beating of a child she was too young to have. Restless, it felt, that child. Little more than a rippling in her belly, but willful enough to make itself known. I remember it well, you see. Sometimes even now I can feel that life in me just the same. When I was young, I believed it was a beginning. I believed nothing could take away a child that could drum so under my skin. And I felt powerful because of it. Little did I understand it wouldn't last.

For years I hadn't seen any boy of your likeness in town. But the last time I went, months ago, before I was bound to this bed, I believed I'd found you in the market, and I hid behind the shelves. There you stood at the counter, that black hair of yours against your skinny frame. What I could see of your face seemed the same as Kyle's, his dark eyelashes and the set of his mouth, as innocent as any child. The boy bought a pack of gum, a set of playing cards, and a pencil. With such a pencil, I thought, a child could write his grandmother. If he knew she existed at all. The boy popped his gum, and Mr. Reed dropped change into his hand. I watched how the man did it. One of his fingers brushing the boy's own in that distracted way people have. He didn't seem to notice. How close he came.

But when that boy turned, I knew he wasn't one of my own. His mouth was too full, his eyes strange. I crouched behind the shelves and felt tired of being wishful. Of looking for anyone who might be my own kin. When I came out from hiding, Mr. Reed seemed to know what I'd been wishing for. He looked me over as I dropped my bread on his counter and said the price as if asking too much. When at last he gave me change, he brushed my fingers with his. That man nodded to me as if that was the best he could do. Knowing you were mine. That I had every right to you. "Good day, Eddie," he said, as if he could understand. Of all my trips to town looking for you, that was my last.

There's no stopping a child from doing what he wants. I know that as well as anyone. My boy, I hope you believe I tried. The next day or the next, I went again with Donny to the Morrows, no matter how he complained. When we turned the final bend, the corral looked quiet. But when the horse stepped through the gate, the dust rose. When Kyle saw us come, he climbed into the corral and took the rope, whipping at the horse to get it running. The boy wanted to impress me, I could tell. But I believe that horse knew what would drive that impression home.

"Kyle," I said, but before I could let out another word, Donny had climbed over the fence and hoisted himself on the animal's back. Then the horse was off. I looked for Kyle to stop it, but Kyle only lifted his hat to me and waved. "Donny, you hear?" I called, pulling myself over the fence. When I stepped into the animal's path and waved my arms, it passed me without a flinch. The animal's flank heaved as it rushed, my son with only two thin reins to hold. Kyle whipped its legs and Donny's mouth opened without a sound. The horse turned about the yard once, twice, Kyle pitching the rope high. The Morrows' house cast a heavy shadow on the yard. It stood large and blank-faced. Not a soul at its lidded windows. Not even Mary looking out. Beyond it, the fields bent under the wind, the leaves on the stalks of corn showed their silver sides, and a haze shivered on the horizon. The corn under that sun, it didn't look natural. And the way my boy clung to the animal seemed desperate and clouded in dust. When the horse circled again, it flung its head. The fence behind me shook and Donny slipped to the horse's side, gripping the mane. Kyle lost hold of the rope and cried out, but still the animal ran. The horse drove Donny against the far fence. It grazed the planks as Donny hung on, the reins knotted now around his hands. It tried to force him off, hanging my son on the fence by his collar as if he were a doll. It raced along that fence over and again, as if the animal couldn't do anything but run, and it trampled Donny when the fence fell.

I should stop myself from telling you this. A child shouldn't know so much. That was the start of your mother's leaving. Eleven as she was herself at the time, as her own brother had been. Two months ago, eleven was your last birthday. Until then, I was hopeful. I made the same pancakes, but with honey and melon this time, and I lit a row of candles. I sat at the end of my table where I could see the clock. *The ocean,* your mother had written just a week before. *Rhode Island,* the stamp said. *It's not so very different,* she wrote. *The way the water looks flat and doesn't change. You'd think there wasn't a thing living in it, but it's terrible how much.* When I looked at a map in town, Rhode Island seemed lost up there in the corner. A state so small and crowded, there didn't seem to be room for a person at all. I wondered why Adaline was going farther still. When she knew how important eleven was and how much I worried. Those candles on the pancakes burned. I lit another row and another. At last I didn't have any more in the box. Sitting at that table, I got to thinking. It's that thinking that put me in this bed. Your mother never did mention you in her letters. I figured she would when she got through being nervous. But eleven should have done it. At eleven, she should have come back. There must have been some reason she didn't. Maybe you never made it to eleven at all.

. . .

It was late in the afternoon when I carried my boy home, though I stayed in our yard to watch over him. When I raised the shawl from my shoulders, the smell bent me double with coughing. I drew the shawl over Donny, head to foot. Behind me, Frank looked out in the coming darkness. He joined me on the grass, touched Donny's leg and drew back. "Sit with me for a while," I said, but I knew Frank wouldn't sit for long. I couldn't imagine how it must be for him, so torn was I with what I'd seen. The way Kyle had whipped the horse's legs. The way the animal had circled, Donny holding on. Frank hugged the boy to his chest.

I would stay crouched on my knees through the night and into the early morning. Every few hours, Frank paced the yard, looking smaller and grayer each time. He never said a word to hurry me. He never so much as scraped his foot on the ground. The fields in front of me blurred. The few clear breaths I took turned to smoke. I dozed where I sat, my head snapping back whenever it fell. Donny and the way he held on. The way he hung from that fence post. When I picked him up, he was hardly more than bones. And when I carried him off, his blood stained the corral. I must have been covered with the same myself.

All this time they'd worried over me, that shawl an omen on my back. Now in my sleep, I saw the fire they'd dreaded. I imagined the fields slapped down by a mighty hand. I thought of the stove we hadn't dared light in the summer and the matches I carried in my pocket. Such a blaze. I knew

I'd seen something like it years ago. Something fantastic and final. A single strike. The match would catch and sputter, making a charred circle in the grass. Soon the shawl over Donny would melt, taking my boy away with it. But I would have to be the one to start it. To save my son from being forgotten. With Donny wrapped in fumes and the heat of the sun rising at my back, I believed I couldn't do otherwise.

XII

Mary

(*Summer 1936*)

What no one knows is how my youngest troubled me, how one look from that boy could stop me where I stood, drop the rag from my hand, and make me take hold of him as if he were innocence itself—can you blame a mother for loving her son? He suffered from gentleness the same as others suffer from waywardness and sin, and I couldn't help but raise him soft, even when he slapped me away, and remind him always of what I knew to be true—that of my sons, he was the one who could be more than the dirt in these fields, that his very blood promised it, even if he pretended at simpleminded ways. He needed only to learn persistence and faith, and these I taught him with a quick word at any misstep, so devoted an eye did I keep on his every doing. But Jack was different. He took a hand to the boy more than he ever had the other two. So Kyle grew quiet, skittish, despite all my efforts to teach him strength. And when I found the boy kneeling on the floor, forced to eat from a broken plate of food he had dropped—my husband standing over him, arms crossed—I swore I would do more than raise him for God. I would raise him a man.

But on that day the horse went wild, Kyle was already half gone. When he came in, he was coated in dust, his hands bleeding and eyes like stones. Without a word, he fell into a chair in a dark corner of my kitchen, head to his knees.

After a time, he said, "Mother, I did something."

"You did nothing," I answered, drying my hands at the sink. "What did you do?"

He shuddered in the chair, the towel twisting in my fingers. Outside, a constant churning of hoofs sounded in the yard and the rush of my husband's footsteps as he yanked open the door.

"Kyle!" Jack called out, as if slapping at the boy's name, but he never did see him huddled in the corner as he was. Without an answer and without seeming to want one, Jack grabbed his shotgun from the wall and went out the way he came. I ran through the door to follow him—even before I knew the reason, he was out in the corral, the horse making desperate circles in the dirt. The fence was down, splintered, a deep, ruddy stain on the wood. The horse struck itself against the far wall, its bony hide red and lathered. With three shots from the gun, the animal fell to the ground.

Inside, I took Kyle's hands and felt the shiver that ran through him before he yanked his hands away. "Where's Dad?" he said.

I shook my head. "You didn't do anything," I whispered to him and whispered it again before Jack was in the room.

"The Current boy," Jack said coming in. I imagined Donny dwarfed in his overalls and hat, twisting his mouth as if riding the horse were a matter of will. I knew that face from his mother, knew it too well. Jack did not offer a word more, but I understood. That horse seemed terribly high next to the boy and still he had ridden it, his hands torn from trying to hold on—I sat on the floor and dropped my head. In the darkness between my knees, my eyes ached. My husband stood above me with his head back, the tanned skin of his neck clutching whenever he swallowed. The gun rested against the table, the smell of burning metal. A groan rose from Kyle's throat and Jack stared.

"It wasn't his doing," I said.

"What?" Jack answered.

"It wasn't him."

"You should have seen it. Jesus, the way Eddie was carrying him." Jack stopped and wiped his mouth. "There'll be talk. If Kyle hadn't let that boy ride it. Hadn't pushed the animal the way he did."

"It wouldn't have mattered. Nothing he ever does—"

"Don't you say it. You know very well why me and that boy have the trouble we do."

Kyle lifted his head and went still, watching us. "It wasn't Kyle," I answered. "Donny wanted to ride the horse, that's all, and that's what we'll say if anyone asks."

Jack's eyes grazed the gun, the table, and the sweating floorboards between us. "You'd do that, wouldn't you?" he started. "You and that church you were always going off to, acting like the good girl." He stopped as if he wanted to say more, but let out a laugh—a low, pained sound, dropping his hands open and slapping his legs. As he left the room, he squeezed Kyle hard on his shoulder before tearing himself away, stomping up the stairs and through the darkness above us. Kyle trembled, looking at the place his father had left. No matter how many times I called his name, the boy never so much as turned his head. So I raised myself from that floor and wiped my cheeks. I rested that gun back on the wall where it belonged—and in the morning before Jack had stirred, before it was quite light, I woke my son from where he had slept the night in that chair and we were gone.

We went straight to the Currents', Kyle lagging so behind that I had to reach back and hurry him, but the boy ignored my hand. He moved as if asleep, quiet and stumbling over the grass. His clothes hung like a scarecrow's from his hips, his arms thin as rails. He had grown far too quickly, without an ounce of fat or muscle—a boy who had seldom heard a kind word from a father in his life. Still Kyle forgave Jack everything, no matter what that man did, while with me he had turned as sullen as his brothers, as if I was the one who had turned Jack against him. Now my eyes watered and I tasted smoke—before us the sky had darkened and just beneath grew a wavering light. The air smelled burnt, a bright flickering where there should have been only corn and beans. Kyle stopped and stared over the plain.

"There's a fire," he shouted. "That's the Currents' fields."

"Kyle?" I yelled out, but the boy had set off. I needed only to talk to Enidina before she saw him again, to convince her that the horse was an accident—but Kyle would make a mess of it, showing himself so recklessly before I even got the chance. Off he went, as if their house still held anything for him, and I could only follow.

It had been seventeen years since I had seen the like, but this fire was different—this I believed was man-made. We hid ourselves from the front of the house, but I could make out Enidina as she crouched in the yard rocking on her knees and Frank standing just behind. The fire was spreading, the corn so dry the leaves shriveled under it, as quick to light as matchsticks. Already the neighboring farmers had driven in. They waited inside their wagons and cars with their doors open, gazing at the corn. It was then I saw the dark bundle on the ground, wrapped as it was in a shawl that burned and smoked after the grass around it had gone out—what had Eddie done? Burnt matches lay scattered around her knees, the earth black. Kyle saw it too and his face broke until he was heaving in the weeds. "Adaline," he muttered and started off, but I caught his arm.

"You've seen enough of that girl," I said.

The heat gusted now against our skin, the fire making us sweat though we stood some distance from it. Enidina clutched her arms to her chest, her eyes shut, indifferent to Frank's hands on her shoulders and the men who had left their wagons now and called to each other for water and sand to put the fire out.

Then Jack was with them—already his face was wet and dark with smoke, signaling the others to work, though they were slow to follow. "What's wrong with you all?" Jack yelled. "Smoke in your ears?" The men broke off from each other and bent to work, steering clear of the large heated man in the middle of them—they would listen to him, their faces said, but they would not like it, glancing off as they did from time to time at the bundle on the ground. Enidina must have heard Jack cursing at them, for she opened her eyes and stood, swaying heavily on her feet. She rushed toward him as if falling, taking him down and striking him weakly with her fists until he yelled and twisted beneath her. Frank gripped her waist and tried to pull her back. "Get her in," the other men were yelling, running toward the scene, but she hauled herself up before they could reach her and they stood back.

It was then she saw Kyle where he hid with me next to the house. She watched him for a time, wavering—there was something in the way she looked, some hungry and half-crazed tremor in her eye. The fire burned behind her, her dress black with soot. She lurched toward us, but I stepped in front of Kyle and slapped her face.

"What's wrong with you, Eddie? Have you gone mad?" Enidina stopped, holding a fist to her ribs.

"It was an accident, Eddie. That's all. Kyle had nothing to do with it."

"It's always you," she said. "You and yours. You're the ones."

Enidina sank to her knees, and the men pushed me aside and carried her into the house. Jack lay on the ground, watching us, and Frank helped him up. "That wife of yours," Jack spit, but Frank stared at him and Jack put up his hands. There were others around us now—the women fleshy and worn with their hair pulled back in handkerchiefs and their eyes red, children squirming in their arms. Their men were squat, ruddy creatures, walking back for buckets and frowning at the rest. Behind them, Borden stepped down from a carriage and a farmer carrying water struck him on the shoulder as he hurried to the fields. "That horse of theirs," the women were saying. "Wild enough to throw a grown man, let alone a boy." Borden stood back, his trousers soaked from the man's buckets. With a sickened look, he turned his head to see the fields and slouched against the carriage wheel. I remembered Kyle behind me and reached back my hand—but when I turned, he was gone.

The door to the house gaped after the men had carried Enidina in. The smoke from the fire darkened the side of the house, but Kyle was nowhere to be found. In the yard, Borden crouched next to the bundle and pulled back the shawl. His hand came away black with char and he stumbled to his feet. Without a glimpse, he rushed past me and caught himself on the porch, wiping his hand against the rail and straightening his jacket before hurrying in. The crowd of neighbors soon lost their interest in me, though they would talk enough in the weeks that followed, saying out loud what they had always wanted to, what they had always thought. "That horse," they would begin. "They should have known. Look at them, always carrying on behind people's backs." I would hear it in the market aisles when none of them thought I was listening and in slips of gossip at church, as if they never had anything better to do with their tongues—and in that talk the horse would become terrible, and my son along with it.

I walked home alone, though I could not help but think of the place where I had borne my son and how we had always been strangers here, what with all their gossip. It had gotten them nothing. Now after the accident, they would study whatever we said or did—if Kyle came back, if he ever showed his face again. But he would never abandon his mother. He would never be so unkind. Over the plain, the wind had grown. An animal bayed in a far-off field and another answered it, the sounds like the calling of a child.

The accident—how could I have forgotten? The fear of it had been sitting just under my skin since Kyle had come into my kitchen, since Jack shot the horse with his gun. I could name it now as I remembered my father's face when he found me, raw-eyed and trembling as I rushed out of the woods. "You won't tell anyone, will you?" the boy had said. "Knowing who my father is. Knowing your father works for him." But my mother never could keep her tongue. The boy's family had been a good deal richer than our own, and she asked them a favor in exchange—a sum to comfort her daughter, a promise of marriage. But the boy's mother had her own way of setting things right—it was entirely my fault, she made clear, inviting the boys out with me in the forest as I did, with a blanket no less. The townspeople turned their backs on us. We were a family of tramps and liars, they said, slandering their community with gossip. Soon they pretended we had never existed at all. That pain between my legs, for so many years it had never left me, and the way those people watched us in Enidina's yard, shunning anything they did not understand. "You and yours," Enidina had said.

Behind me the fire was lessening, the wind grew quiet as the heat died, but not a soul worried the horizon, not even an animal in its pasture. A dust rose up ahead and I imagined Enidina running toward that horse with Donny on its back, the way it bucked against that look on her face. I could pretend I had seen it myself, from my place at the window where I so often looked out. And if I repeated the story often enough, if I imagined every part, I might begin to remember it just that way—not an accident at all, but a part of Enidina's carelessness, how she had rushed at that horse with her fists and spooked it, sending the poor animal off in a wild run around the yard and throwing the boy in fear for itself. There were far more terrible things than pretending, I knew that much—far more terrible than telling something different. Enidina had been the one to make the horse buck, not my son. And with such a story, I could stop Kyle from running, as his own brothers had run before him. I could find some way to quiet people's tongues and keep him safe—but Kyle would have to help. I would need to convince him myself when I returned home.

The house was the same as I had left it, the gun on the wall, the towel by the sink, the chair pulled into the dark corner of my kitchen, but the chair was empty now, as was the house. The gaping ship glared back at me as I walked the rooms. Even Jack was gone—I would find him later in the early morning, lying straight on his back in the barn, breathing as he did when he was asleep, that great rumbling that ran through him. My husband slept like a man who no longer enjoyed sleeping, who found no release in it, and lately he had lived like a beast tossing in circles in its stall—he would not return to our bed until the night he died.

I found Kyle's door shut the next evening and turned the knob. "Kyle," I called. He sat on his bed, head in his hands, and I lifted his chin—his cheeks were bloodied and dark.

"What did they do?"

He dropped his head.

"Kyle, things like this can be terrible for a family. There are consequences. You don't understand what people are capable of."

"He died," he said. Delicate as he was, he sat with his knees nearly to his ears in a mess of sheets.

"Donny," I said.

"He's dead."

"You don't have to keep repeating it."

"But that's all I am. To her, that's it."

I stood from the bed and straightened my skirts. I did not know this "her" he spoke of—I thought he might even have meant me. Outside his window, the Currents' house was a white-headed pin, the fields surrounding it black and crushed like a piece of coal. "That poor boy isn't all there is," I said. "There are others to think about. Your father and your brothers, for one. Me."

Kyle made a strange, sobbing sound and dropped back in his bed, covering his face. "What did he mean? That thing Dad said. 'You know very well.'"

"He didn't know what he was saying, Kyle. He was in one of his fits."

"This was different."

"It was worse, that's all. Your father takes no pleasure in shooting a horse."

Kyle went quiet.

"Listen, there's no way to undo what happened, but you should consider your family now. There are things we need to make happen. People we have to convince. Our way of seeing it, that's what matters . . ."

"All right, Mother," he whispered between his teeth.

"But you have to agree . . ."

"I said all right."

He lay on the bed and his chest rose and fell, his lip swollen as if he had been punched and his hands raw with scratches. I closed his door behind me but listened for him through the wall. I would have to speak to him again—I would have to be more forceful. Kyle had always been so restless, the thought of keeping still like death to him, as if he hoped the truth of this world would not reveal itself as long as he kept going. "Mother?" he called from the other side of the door, and I took my ear away. "What are you going to do?" But I was not ready for explanations—not then. I made my way down the stairs and could still hear him at my back, opening his door and asking questions. *What did he mean?* It was the way he had said it, as if I kept some secret about Jack from him—but I never did, not anything I cared then or later to tell him. And until this day, I have never said a word.

XIII

Enidina

(Summer 1936–Spring 1937)

They brought me to my mother's after the fire. I'd asked
Frank for this while I lay in my bed that afternoon, listening
to the fire outside dampen and the calls of the men. Frank
was sweating as he held my hand. He said our house would
be safe, the fire had turned and was heading down the field.
Outside, the men worked to remedy what I'd begun. The
doctor claimed me cured of my fevers. He told Frank, "Take
her to her mother's. It's all she wants."

In a borrowed car, Frank drove me to her home and my
Adaline came with me. I felt sick with moving so fast, used
as I was to wagons even then. I tried to think of something
slow and remembered leaning against my mother's leg as
a child. Back then, at the turn of the century, all the world
seemed to be breaking apart. Many were looking for the
Second Coming. Some even took their own lives. In the
summer of 1899, our town seemed to close up altogether.
Houses emptied or fell silent, the people inside losing
themselves one way or another. Poisons, rope, blades, or
drowning. But never the grandmothers, it seemed. Never
the old. Then the last of it, the wife who'd lost three children to fevers from the winter before. Without a penny in
her pocket or so much as a loaf of bread in a paper sack,
she left town on foot. The ones who saw her go said she

walked without hurry, as if she had a destination well in mind. She kept her eyes on the horizon. She never wavered. Never looked back. When they found her weeks later, she had gone more than a hundred miles and dropped to her knees when she grew tired. She had died like that.

My father was done with religion then and kept us from church, but my mother read her Bible when she wanted. Sitting on the floor at her feet, I could smell her lap, warm and damp under her dress. I'd rarely been so close. What I'd heard about the woman who walked away and all the rest troubled me, and I asked her would He come.

My mother answered by stopping her work and tapping her Bible on the table next to her chair. "Nothing like that's to happen to us," she said. "Not anytime before the year 1939." She looked up through the ceiling and I couldn't see her face. Her neck was marbled with veins. "And you have to believe that, Enidina. It's written down and has been for some time." My mother grew quiet then and went back to her stitching. She had saved her rags and the rags of her neighbors in a basket at her side. Now she smoothed them into strips and pieced them together. Those rugs she made, they were just like my grandmother's. Like the ones my mother tried to teach me. Braiding them, it's how women told each other things. She started with something old, something others thought rubbish, but what she stitched spilled out from her neat and warm and wanting of a house. When I saw each rug she made, with no holes or loose stitching, I believed she knew of such matters. She knew the ways of a thing breaking apart and she knew how to fix it and she was holding the Coming off from our house until the year 1939.

But in the days after the fire, I had my doubts. Nineteen thirty-nine was only three years off. My dress was dark with smoke and still reeked of it. In our yard I'd waited too close to see how my son went. Walking into my mother's house, I carried his smoke in with me. My mother sat stitching in her chair, but Adaline pulled at her until the rags she worked slipped out of her hands.

"Where's the other one?" my mother asked.

It was Frank who answered, standing at the door as he was. "There was a fire," he said. Without a sound, he had come in and dropped our bags on the floor. I never thought a person could grieve in so much quiet. My boy, I feared I'd lost him with what I'd done. But when Frank touched my arm in my mother's house, he let his hand rest there for a while and warm the both of us. Finally he said he had to go.

I stood in the light of the doorway as the car pulled onto the road. Looking back, Frank lifted his hand to me and let it fall. My mother caught hold of Adaline and tried to settle her, but she only loosened the rags from my daughter's grip. The girl tore around the room, upsetting the piano bench, and my mother took the rags in her fists and kissed them, pressing them roughly against her cheeks. Up the stairs Adaline went, roaring above us and banging every door. Outside the sun was setting and the house felt close in the coming darkness. Night would be a relief to me. That morning I'd seen such a bright hot thing in the field. I didn't know what I'd done or what would come of it. I only knew it came from me.

I sat on my mother's floor again and leaned against her legs. She went back to her stitching, though her hands shook with grief. She was going blind, my mother. The neighbors no longer wanted the rugs they'd paid for, the colors now a bright and curious mix of her own choosing. They had to give them away. Still, they were fine pieces of work. Smooth and careful in their stitching. "Is it now?" I asked as her fingers turned. I was sleepy and in the dark room what I believed of any Second Coming seemed fit for the morning. I coughed with the smoke still clinging to me and reached around my shoulders, but the shawl was no longer there.

My mother kept at her rags, clearing her throat as if to convince herself. "Children die, Eddie. It's not God who does it." Her eyes grew wet and she blinked. Taking hold of my hands, she kissed them, and I wondered if she could taste the salt that stained my cheeks. Above us, Adaline ran in a fury down the hall. I remembered how I'd felt for the matches in my apron early that morning. It was fire I'd been dreaming of, keeping vigil as I did that night outside with my son. I dropped one match and the ground took the flame, the stalks going with it. In my fever, the fire spread faster than I could have imagined. When finally I turned back to the house, there was your mother at her window, gripping the sill. How I'd hoped to save her from that sight. How sure I was that no other burial would do for my son. But Donny had always been more his sister's child than my own.

"You've got to watch out for her now," my mother said. "She'll slip away from you quick as rain. Keep her close." She looked at her stitching again and measured the rug against her chest. "This is for you, Eddie," she said, folding the rug across my knees. "For when you go home."

. . .

Two days later the trucks still lined the road in front of our house, our neighbors crowding in. They were curious to see the fields and to see where the fire had stopped at the ditches along the road. It didn't spread to anyone else's land. None of them had suffered a loss to complain about. Leaning out their husbands' windows, the women hooked their elbows over the doors, and the children peeked through the passengers' sides, sometimes three heads together. The men waited by their tires or gathered in a circle, watching as we passed by. I suppose that was what they'd come for.

Most of our crop was gone. The stalks stood like spent torches or lay broken in the soil. The trucks crowded each other, but now none of the men would set foot in the fields, afraid whatever fever had caused the fire might spread to wives of their own. We pulled into our yard and I touched my feet to the ground. I could smell it again, the fire, the burnt-up corn, and the animals, safe in the barn. They were quiet now. Though their pails were full, Frank said they wouldn't eat. In time, he figured, they would grow hungry enough. All at once the trucks started their engines. The roar echoed against our house, all of it noise.

When we stepped in, Mary was there again and I wasn't surprised to see her. She stood over the stove wearing my apron, a towel in her hand and her hair tucked behind her ears. I watched her warily. When she opened the stove, it sent out such a heat that we all fell into place at the table and didn't speak. For the first time in days, even Adaline was quiet. She rested her head against her father's chest and he drew his arm around her, his mouth working at something he was holding back. Since the drive from my mother's place, he hadn't yet said a word.

Mary set out our plates and left a pile of forks and knives between us. She poked her fork into a potato on the stove and the fork went easily through. Her face was red with the heat and fallen. Her cheeks, her mouth. She seemed older now, and the corner of her eye twitched. My face still stung from Mary's hand. I'd said something cruel and meant it. "You and yours," I'd said. But except for that twitch Mary seemed too wearied now to do anything at all. She rolled the potatoes onto our plates and we stared at them between our empty hands. When finally she bowed her head to bless the meal, I couldn't even close my eyes.

"Nice of you," I said when she'd finished. She was a mother too, I reminded myself.

"Yes," Mary answered.

"Nice this." My potato steamed as I broke the skin, and Mary watched us as we ate, fork in hand. "Your middle son," I tried again. "I heard he went west."

"My son?"

"Yes."

"Well, yes he did." Mary lifted her chin. "And the other one. The oldest. You should see him. He's in Chicago now. There are bread lines, you know. But Chicago . . ."

"So far off."

"He says it's the place to be."

I lifted a piece of potato, blew on it, and took a bite. Before the fire, it'd been a long time since I'd spoken to Mary. Longer than I'd realized. But the Morrows were different from us. I still had the scars from Jack's knife and the way he'd shown up in our fields after the fire, as if he owned the place.

"Kyle send that animal off yet?" Frank said. "Like I told him?" He kept his eyes on his plate, his mouth full.

"Jack took care of it days ago. He's quick with his gun."

Frank swallowed and sat back. "That wasn't called for. That wasn't called for at all." Mary salted her potato as if she didn't hear and Frank went back to his meal, working his jaw. We were quiet, scraping food from our plates. Mary set a pitcher of water on the table and we drank fast from our cups. It was too hot an afternoon for baking, but the potatoes settled us. It was the first time in days I'd had an appetite myself.

"I don't know what he told you," Mary started. "Borden, he went to you first."

"That's what ministers are for," Frank told her.

"He didn't say much," I added. Or I didn't remember what he said, I thought. The twins, that's what I had my mind on then. Borden seemed too nervous a man to do much of anything useful.

"He almost died himself when he was that age. That's what he said," Frank explained. "He didn't understand it. Why one and not the other. There had to be a way to make it right, he thought."

Mary held on to her water glass though it was empty, that twitch again at the corner of her eye. I thought of the twins when they were younger and how we'd raked leaves in the fall. We swept them into piles that Adaline and Donny couldn't help themselves from jumping in. When at last we had one great pile together, we set it on fire. Frank stood watch, digging into the fire with his rake. At the sink inside, I washed potatoes and could see him out there, spare and long-limbed, the air about him wavering. I gave four potatoes each to the children, grinning. "Throw them on top of the leaves," I said.

Donny and Adaline ran with their arms full to the fire. But when they reached it, they held those potatoes tight. They must have thought it was burning up food to do such a thing. I stepped out into the yard and yelled, "Go on." They threw the potatoes then with both hands, jumping with the effort, their arms high over their heads. The potatoes flew. I thought they'd miss the pile entirely, but they landed in the middle with a thump.

"You're leaving," Mary announced. "You have to." She had both her elbows on the table, pointing her fork. "It will be easy for you. We can buy the fields."

You can leave potatoes in a fire like that until the fire has died. Until there is a black circle in the grass and the potatoes sit inside like coals. Brush the ashes off and the potatoes will taste like the grass and soil they come from. Like the good smell of the fire you try to keep inside your clothes. But this you can eat. You can hold it in your mouth as if you are holding on to everything at once. When you swallow it, you belong to that place and that fire. My boy, you have it in you always.

"Eddie," Mary snapped. "It would be good of you at least to apologize for what you've done. You don't know what they're saying."

I rested my hands in my lap and thought about that, Mary speaking with her knife. I should have found a way to keep my son a little. But it was a relief, that fire. It took him straight away. There wouldn't be any work to bury him. There wouldn't be a mound in the yard marked by a stone. I felt an awful rush in my head. Mary was on her feet. That twitch. Whether we left or not, she'd already made her mind up about what she'd do next. I remembered that slap again. Cruel, what I'd said. But I doubted I was wrong.

"Why'd you come, Mary?"

"I wanted to tell you."

"Why?"

"Because I know what they'll do and I can't stop it. People think you've gone near crazy and they want to make sure nothing like this happens again."

Frank stood and the table jumped an inch across the floor. Pulling at Mary's arm, he took her straight out of our house to where her car waited in the road. He sat her in it and shut the door behind her, catching the end of her skirt. When she opened the door again, her mouth was quivering, and she snatched at her hem. "Just you think about it," she called out. "Before someone takes advantage."

Adaline slumped against her father's chair and murmured as she dreamed. The buttons of Frank's shirt had left their mark on her cheek. I swept a strand of hair from her forehead, desperate as she looked. Borden had come to give us some peace, I knew. But he was not a peaceful man. He'd sat next to me in our front room and wouldn't look me in the eye. Why one and not the other, that's what he'd said. But it wasn't the kind of question a person asked. Not anyone with common sense. There are no good reasons for life or death. And no decent God could even begin to make a choice. Outside, Mary sat watching the house. I knew she was up to something, and now I believed Borden might be a part. Frank waited at the door outside, pinching his hat between his fingers until he was sure she was well sent off. At last she drove away.

I lay my head on the table, but I couldn't rest. I felt terrible for Frank and your mother both. Frank stood in the doorway with a heavy head and didn't look back. When smoke rose from the stove, I opened the lid with my bare hand. Mary had left two potatoes inside and they looked burnt through, their skins as black and tight as stones. Taking them out, I burnt my fingers to blistering. But when I cut into that bitter crust, the potatoes underneath were good and soft and white.

She was our only one then, your mother, and she was always trying to fill the quiet. Snapping her fingers, banging cabinets, taking down the house all by herself. Or so I reminded her. But her eyes rarely settled on either of us any more. We left the door to our house open to let her out. Hours she spent in the fields and beyond the road, rolling marbles or dice, jumping hopscotch over squares she drew with a stick in the dust. She had long talks with imaginary friends, scolding them with a shake of her finger. In the corn she hid herself and found herself and sought herself out, staying there all day with her games. No one let the other children come near.

But at night there was only the one attic room she'd slept in with her brother and the memory of him going to the outhouse at least twice a night, keeping her awake. After the fire, that attic must have felt full of his being gone.

It wasn't for weeks until Kyle came himself. He waited in our yard, staring at the house for any sign of the girl. He must have believed taking a step closer would do us another wrong. But from where I watched, I thought of inviting him in. I thought of taking hold of him and wringing out everything that had happened.

"Addie," he said when he saw her.

She'd walked in from the field, but when she noticed him there, she stopped. I remembered how I'd found him in our house after Borden had left, with everyone else still in the yard. He lay on his back with a bloodied nose, my daughter with her knees against his stomach, holding him down. Her cheeks were streaked, a sound like a cat in her throat. As I pulled her back, Adaline kicked and spit, but as soon as I put her to bed, she quieted. When I came out again, Kyle still lay on our floor in the hall, his eyes shut. I lifted him up, but I didn't have the heart to tend to him. Not the way I once did.

Now in our yard, Adaline's knuckles were red and broken from her beating on him. "Don't," he said as if fearing the same.

"What do you want?"

"To see you."

"Who says I want to be seen?"

"Well, I guess not." Kyle hid his hands in his pockets and seemed about to spit. The rose in Adaline's cheeks came from her time in the fields, though it was stronger now. Her black hair fell loose in the daylight, her ankles bare.

Her coral dress with its thin straps showed the lines of sun on her skin. I felt nervous for her, the woman she was becoming in the clothes of a girl. But before I could send Kyle home, Adaline kicked the dirt and left him in a cloud of dust.

"Hey," he said.

"Hey what?" Adaline kicked the dirt again.

"Hey," he shouted and seized her arm. She twisted his hand behind his back, and he bent to the ground, laughing. Adaline's face was furious, glowing. They scuffled in the dirt until they were covered. Finally Kyle twisted himself right and pressed her arm against his chest. "Listen," he said.

But Adaline kicked the dirt again, harder this time.

Kyle let go of her arm and fixed his hat on his head, trying to smile. "Ever wonder what it might be like to leave this place?"

Adaline stared at him.

"I'm thinking about it," he said. "About leaving."

"So?"

"That's all you've got to say?"

She lunged at him and slapped his face. He stumbled. The two squared off against each other again, my girl only half his size though fierce in the fury of all her eleven years. She snatched the hat off his head and ran inside the house, leaving Kyle looking close to naked in our yard. I asked her what went wrong.

"Nothing," she said, though her eyes brimmed. She dropped the hat at my feet. "I hate this place. I hate everything about it. It's all just going away."

She ran up the stairs and slammed her door. Out the window, Kyle stood with his arms limp, hair stuck to his scalp. It was then I saw Mary, waiting as she did down the road a good distance. As if she had any right to watch us. Kyle turned toward home though he didn't raise his head to his mother as he passed her. She seized his sleeve, but he wrenched away, leaving her to stare after him. When she turned at last to our house, her look was desperate. I feared what she might do after Kyle had come to our place and still wanted to be a part of it. After everything else, he'd done that. And I didn't have to imagine how she felt.

My boy, I suppose any mention of your parents might be hard to take. But before I lose my strength, I want to get this down whether it's useful or not. There were both things between your parents after the fire, their easy way as children and Donny's accident. It was Kyle's horse, Kyle's goading that had gotten my son on the animal. And it was Kyle who'd whipped at the horse to get it going. But Adaline was lonely after the loss of her brother, and your father didn't leave this place. Not until Jack himself was gone. No matter what I imagined might happen between that boy and Adaline, I kept my peace. I didn't want to lose another child.

I study the nurse where she sits now in my chair, her lips moving. I can't understand a thing she says. But that twitch of hers, it tells enough. "Who sent you?" I ask.

"County services," she says. I know her and it's been for more than the last few months, what with her white hair pulled back, the way her foot sticks out when she crosses her legs.

"Whose?"

"The county."

I stay quiet. I can only think about asking her again.

"Look," she starts. "There must be an address on one of those letters."

"Why?"

"It would be good for you," she says. "To have your family here. People who know you. Who can take care of you. Don't you want your daughter back? Your son-in-law?"

"That letter they sent," I say. It's all her talk about family, the way she keeps after me, and I can imagine the pages of that letter again. It came more than eleven years ago. Of that I'm certain. I burnt it as soon as I could.

The nurse grips her hands in her lap and her heel jerks. "You don't want to tell me, do you? Because that way, I could write too."

"That letter was the last thing."

"I don't know what you're talking about."

"Frank never got over it. And the ones who sent it, they pretended they were good people, the praying kind."

"You're sleeping too much. Confusing things."

"She was trying to keep Kyle from leaving."

"You're not listening."

"But that boy was always going to go. No matter what she did, it was a waste." My eyes blur, a rush of heat in my cheeks. Then I can't remember why I've said it or what it was, wasted or not. All of it must have been before Adaline left.

"That's a long time ago," the nurse says, but her heel has stopped now. Both her feet are on the floor. I close my eyes and hear the scrape of her chair, a blanket pulled to my chin. Letters, I think. Before the nurse leaves, she takes the box again from under the bed and searches through. But she won't find anything close to an address. I never did.

XIV

Mary

(*Summer 1936*)

I left for the church early enough in the morning so I could not change my mind. *She set that fire,* I planned to remind Borden. *Burned that boy right along with everything else*—and the rest of it, that I had found Enidina watching Kyle with his horse only days before, crouched behind our old winter fences, her prying certain to have made the horse jumpy. I had seen the accident myself, I would say—and Borden would hear it, hands in his lap—the way Enidina worked the animal up and insisted on holding the rope, though the horse never did know her, had become nervous with her very presence. It was no fault of the animal, gentle as it was, no fault of my son—Enidina herself had made the horse buck. The steeple appeared small and far in the countryside, and a buzzing sounded in my ears. I hurried my steps. Even if what I told him was not true, I thought, it seemed the kind of story that could set things right. *Some might think it's interesting how similar you and my son look,* I would finish if he had any doubt. *If I said a word, some might think a man of God had taken advantage.*

"The way to goodness," Borden had said, but this before Kyle was born, when I sat crouching with those women in the basement of the church, weaving wreaths for the Christmas service, my hands bloody with the work. "Mary," he had said. "You should have worn gloves." The women scattered, leaving Borden alone to take his handkerchief from his pocket. "I thought you might play," he said. "Since you're here, I mean." His voice was little more than a whisper, and I raised my head—but he did not take his eyes from that handkerchief, pressing my fingers between his.

That chapel, I remember it as nearly glowing no matter what time of day, smelling of wax and warm wood, the plush red tongue of the carpet spilling down the center aisle. God himself watched over it, I was sure, the walls keeping out the wind and any sound from the world outside. When the roof escaped a lightning strike that burned the limb of a nearby tree, it was God's doing, leaving only a patch of earth where the grass would not grow. God was there in the worst of storms, lifting the gutters from the rain like a woman lifting her skirts—and as I walked down the aisle to play the piano, Borden close at my back, I knew God was there too.

"It's not enough," my mother used to say, and now I understood what she meant—a husband and two sons, a house of our own, and the farm we worked. My husband left every morning for the fields with his cheeks full of biscuits, a hat on his head, and the stove still warm at my back. With a wave of his hand he was gone, nothing for the daylight hours but weeds in my garden and canning in the kitchen, the bony shoulders of my sons for comfort.

It was never enough—I felt sick thinking about it and stopped before we had reached the front of the church, Borden's presence warm on the back of my neck. The pulpit stood beneath a heavy cross, the place restless and strange without its members. In the worn suit he seemed to wear every hour of every day, Borden looked unsteady on his feet, a tuft of hair standing from his forehead. I wet my finger—God was there, I believed, and whatever I wanted in this church and on that farm I could have all at once, and the two could sustain each other, like the two sides of a coin, and I should never question it. I swept the hair back into place and Borden blinked. Why had I never noticed before, the way the fine hair on his temples faded to a white near his skin?

I sat at the piano and the bench shifted as Borden sat next to me.

"I take requests."

"Whatever you want," he said. His knees hit the wood under the keyboard as he tried to fit his legs. "There was an elderly man here last week," he went on. "Marvin Kindel. He had traveled to twelve states, and the churches were always the friendliest places. Better than barrooms, he said. In a church, there was always a man you could discuss the deepest matters with. But the whole time he talked, I couldn't stop looking at his shoes. They were bright yellow, some kind of boots. He was probably in his eighties and barely came to my chin, though at one time he must have been a large man. He was the loneliest person I've ever met."

I looked at him, my fingers on the piano but not playing, my elbow resting against his arm. Twice now he had told me about strangers—as if he believed he would cease to exist if no one came to the church asking for him, as if asking was all he ever got. "How did it happen?" I said, pointing to his leg.

"My father," he said, shrugging. "It was his first try at building a church. I was twelve, helping him. A beam fell. My mother didn't let him finish the church after that. She wouldn't let him build another one either, not while she was living. When she died, my father came here. I was the reason he waited so long."

Borden dropped his fingers to the keys, a dull twang. The skin on his wrist seemed paper thin, lined with veins, and the muscles twitched. "No one's ever asked," he said. The rush I felt under my ribs, it had not left me, not when his coat settled against my hip or now as I listened—he talked about wives who worried over restless husbands, widows who brought dishes hot from the stove. When finally he grew quiet, I started to play, but my fingertips ached when I touched the keys, the ivory beneath dark with bloody prints. Borden folded my hands into the corner of his jacket and held them against his hip as we sat, the piano humming still. For a long while we sat like that, resting against each other. I believed he would never let go.

It must have been the same for my youngest boy—Adaline and the way she looked, those dresses too small for her and her back pliable as grass, twisting her foot out and still stinking of the farm. She was a fire, that girl, with Frank's thinness and good looks and a vein of steel like her mother. She should have been born a boulder, just like that woman, but she was lovely—despite all her roughness—more than any other girl in town. Though my son could turn heads when he walked through the streets, though the ladies commented on his sweetness and charm, Adaline's looks made her dangerous, especially for my son—there was a loneliness to her now that sent waves, living out on that farm with no one her age for company, no one who would even come near.

Of course I have imagined how it went, ever since the day I found that blanket in the Currents' northmost field—months after they had run off. It was a mangy pile of wool, so dirty I could not carry it home without coughing, and I shut it away in my closet, still ripe. I doubt they minded that stink themselves, young as they were and desperate enough to be out there to begin with. I had once known such desperateness, no matter how short-lived—but it was that girl who had made it stick, who had gotten away from this place. That kind of desperate, it can turn a woman reckless with any man who asks.

I had seen Adaline myself from my kitchen window the day she watched Kyle in the fields. There she stood with her bare arms hooked over our gate, Kyle riding the tractor a good stone's throw away, working closer to her row by row. He frowned, turned the engine off, and dropped to the ground, looking for some trouble between the wheels. He never did belong in this place, Adaline must have thought, that dust making him squint, the sun difficult. When Kyle saw her at last, he stopped where he stood. Adaline wore an old straw hat, one of Jack's that Kyle himself had taken long before and soon after lost. The hat sat crookedly on her head, the brim fallen to her nose, and she pushed it back with a wink. Kyle never smiled. He never waved. He never said a word—he only watched her like a wild bird he might scare off. Finally he turned his back and climbed into his seat. When he looked for her again, Adaline was gone, that hat twirling on the gatepost for him. The next day or the next, they met at that corner of our road as if they had somehow agreed.

It must have been late in the afternoon when they found it—that patch of dirt in the fields they soon thought of as their own, where out of a strange sort of indifference nothing grew and the corn stood like walls. The soil lay flat, the earth cool against their backs as they looked up at the sky overhead—like falling it must have felt, and she gripped his hand. "Kyle," she must have said. She liked to say it now because it was different from the way his name had sounded to her before. It curled her tongue, like biting the meat from an orange—before he was just a boy and his name never sounded like anything at all.

He leaned close enough to touch her bare shoulder with his, his skinny legs sticking out under the worn denim overalls, much longer than her own limbs. She must have thought him good-looking, my son, with those sharp cheekbones, as if he were starved. More than that, she must have liked that smell on him, the sticky saltiness like the belly of a dog, but harder somehow, finer, and sharp to the tongue. His hand fit into the small of her back, as if that was where it had come from.

"We're not supposed to be here," he said.

She leaned so close he could almost rest his chin in the curls on her head. It was a dare, he thought.

"Where are we supposed to be?"

Her hands were small, the bones of a bird—he could have smelled the cows on her and touched the white scattering of hair that clung to her skirt, making her familiar and warm and as easy as mornings in the barn. Such a girl—with her blue-black hair and her quickness, the way she never shied from anything. Who knew what kind of fire she had in her? What that look of hers promised?

"I thought you might play," Borden had said. Still gripping my hands, he rose from the bench and took me down the hall to his rooms. I had never seen such a sad place, a single cot with white linens, a scabby desk and chair that tried to match. The room smelled of paper and dust, pages of sermons pinned to the walls with *X*'s through the paragraphs— *We are not the only ones who must know God*, he had scrawled at the bottom of a page, beneath line after line of scratched-out sentences. "Sit," he said, and I found myself in the nest of sheets on his bed. *We are not the only ones*, I thought, but those sheets were simple and soft, tossed aside as if he had only just slept in them and smelling of that sleep. Borden bent to his knees and took off my shoes, gripping my feet. He pressed his hand against my neck and slid his fingers down my collarbone. God would understand such things, I believed. Ecstasy and passion, they were God's doing, and forgiveness was God's. Everything was. Already I could see it on Borden's face, a kind of light, a blessedness—and as he pressed into me in that nest of sheets, I knew that blessedness was ours.

. . .

It was only days after the Currents' fire when I stood in that church again, but the chapel had suffered years of aging, something I could not recognize until it lay empty now and quiet. The wooden steps were unpainted and rotting. The walls had faded to a dirty white. Borden sat in the front pew, pale as the walls and thin, so much smaller than I remembered, and he raised his eyes at my presence. *Some might think*, I would say—I would make myself the center of the story. If I convinced him, no one could say a word against us. I sat in the pew beside him and gripped his hand—how good and warm that hand was, though stiffer than it once had been, and I thought of what that hand meant, what it had always promised.

"How is she?" he asked.

"Who?"

"Enidina. Isn't that why you're here?"

I sat back against the hard wood. "I'm here about Kyle."

Borden pulled his hand from mine, but I took it again and held it more fiercely in my lap.

"I have no ownership of that boy," he said. "Jack is his father. I'm nothing to him."

"Why did you go to her first?" I asked.

"Why wouldn't I? Eddie lost a son."

"You have a son you can lose too."

"I go where I'm expected. Where I do the most good."

"You owe us."

"I can't do anything about that."

"Just believe my side of the story. If anyone asks about Kyle's horse, tell them it was Enidina all along."

"I don't know what you're talking about."

"I never expected anything from you, did I? All this time. I let you go, pretending whatever you wanted."

"What did I pretend?"

"You pretended plenty."

He flinched, but still I held his hand. He is an old man, I thought, little more than fifty, but he creaks like this bench when he talks. I tried to think of him as he was when he was young—that look on his face and the way he trembled. I had to think of that to speak to him at all.

"You can't come in here like this," he said.

"They'll start talking, don't you see?" I went on. "If you don't do something, I will."

"What will you do?"

"Pretending you didn't even know me. A man of God, as if you'd never touched a woman in your life. What do you think they'll say when I tell them? You won't have a church at all."

Borden tore his hand from mine, and the light in the chapel went strange. He was nothing like he had been, now with his voice rising and the veins breaking across his cheeks. This man I believed I had known so well—with his clean, white skin, his faulty gait, and the shock of black hair under his collar—how had he kept out of the sun and dust and trouble of this place for so long? Jack wouldn't have ignored me the way this man did. Jack never ignored anything.

I closed my eyes and tried to think, but it was Jack I remembered and the look on his face in our kitchen years ago, the first time he brought me oranges from the store—an unusual gift at the time, what with their bright skin. The boys turned the oranges in their hands but would not eat them. Jack showed them how to peel the fruit with their fingers, pulling back the skin where the undersides showed a snowy white, and the sharp smell made the boys laugh. He dug his thumb into the meat and split the orange into pieces, giving one to each, and the boys ate them with juice on their chins. When Jack peeled the last one and held a piece to my mouth, I felt the coarse skin of his fingertips and tasted the salt and heat of his work with the fruit's sweetness—so wild a taste I found myself asking for another piece from his hands.

"Mary," Borden broke in. I opened my eyes and he had moved away, standing now behind a high wooden bench and clutching one of his books. "You can't expect so much," he said. It is years ago now, but I can still feel Jack as he was that last night in our bed. What had woken me to his presence was not his new weight after all those years or any sound he had made coming in after dark. In my sleep, he had taken hold of my wrist, so tight that when he died and loosened his grip, the blood that rushed to my fingers felt painful and alive.

"I won't be forced into describing something the way it isn't," Borden was saying. "Not any more." He would not look at me as he went on, about people and their expectations, about the decency of letting things go—but I no longer listened. I could think only of my husband, that juice on his hands. My visit to the church was long before Jack died, but even then I sensed that I was the one who had made Jack what he was, every last violent step. Borden stood before me, pretending to take offense, but the way he looked over the pews, I could tell he was thinking something different. If our letter to Enidina helped anyone, it was Borden, the congregation seized by his mission, the righting of a wrong. The next time I saw him at the pulpit, the man had grown gaunt with worry—but the congregation was with him again, the offering plates heavy, and his father's church full. He would live on in that church for years until one day the congregation found the doors locked, the place empty— the man who had been their faithful minister disappeared without any sign of having ever been there at all.

You may believe my going to the church was the worst, I would try to tell Kyle in a letter years later, one of the many he never got. So many pages have I written without a word back—there are stacks of them on the table, gray with dust, and stacks near my chair as high as my hip. RETURN TO SENDER, they say, with the stamp of that severed hand pointing off. That boy disappeared from this place soon after Jack died, as if the only good reason for his running had not already left the only way a man like Jack knew how. *You don't know what they could have done to us,* I wrote. *You don't know how many teeth that gossip had in it . . .* , but I never could explain what I did. "Someday you'll know better," my father had said, and that boy in the woods with me, catching me in his fists. I remember how dizzy I had been whenever I was touched, and how that dizziness first reared its head when I was leaving those woods for the last time. The boy's hand across my mouth, the bitter scent—how the town turned against us instead of the one who had done worse. "My God," Jack complained. "I know what it means." There were all those things, the boy in the woods, the knife between my legs, and the way Jack had never forgiven me, the cold feeling in the church years later and the look on Borden's face, as if I meant nothing to him. *You can't expect your old mother to wait for so long,* I wrote to Kyle, hoping he might come home. *It's different without Jack. You could make a new kind of life in this place if only you'd try . . .*

I walked home alone from the church. In my tiredness I called out to Kyle to let me in. My youngest shuffled down the stairs in the darkness, but left me alone once inside. What I had done was for him, but I lost him all the same—though I would not know the truth of it for years. That night after my visit, I dreamed the church was as new as the day I had found it, with the young stranger speaking my name. That place was the farthest I ever went. I stayed late in the afternoons when I could, when the winters made walking home difficult—and then there was Kyle. That night, I imagined it whitewashed again and brilliant, smelling of grace, and when I walked into the chapel, there was Borden, without that darkness in his eyes or a hint of impatience, without looking away. When I lifted my hands, he was there to catch them, touching my fingers to his lips.

"It's the Currents' fault," I told him. "Their boy, Donny. They're the ones."

XV

Enidina

(*Summer 1937–Fall 1939*)

When the letter arrived, we were expecting it. Sitting in our box on the other side of the road, it'd been delivered on foot. We didn't have to wonder which of our neighbors had walked out there on her thin heels and left it for us. *As you have been dishonest,* it started. *In your ways of achieving financial success.* The paper was tissue thin. The lettering strict. The congregation had signed their names at the bottom like a stamp.

The summer after the fire, our field had grown. It had grown the next year and the year after that, better than any of our neighbors'. With the money that came in, we braced the barn. Bought back the acres we'd lost to the droughts. Frank put gaslights in the house and bought us a car. One of the finest cars in town he bought, but only because he believed it would last. Adaline swept her hands over the hood and helped her father wash it, but mostly she kept to herself. The stalks she hid in straightened over her head. The fields grew up finer than ever, your mother becoming beautiful in their midst. For a time I believed the way our life had been might come back to us, that we might make a fine living again. If only we could stay in one piece.

But the fire had changed things. The town was different. The people had grown quiet, their manners easy, except when they thought we weren't looking. The clerks wouldn't name a price, writing it instead on a slip of paper and pushing the paper across. We sat as we always did at the back of the church, but no one but drifters sat with us now. That's when I knew. The way the others kept their backs turned, all but ignoring us during greetings before service. There must have been meetings. Votes we weren't invited to attend. Between us and the front of that church, a great crowd had joined together and left us out.

"What have you done?" Mary read from the podium. She stood with the Bible at her breast, but the stories she told sounded different from any scripture I'd heard before. Borden sat on his bench behind her, head nearly in his lap. "Now you are under a curse," Mary read. "Driven from the ground. When you work the land, it will no longer yield you crops. You will be a wanderer on earth for the rest of your life."

My boy, there are more ways than one to send a person wandering. It doesn't take much to become a stranger in your own home. It wouldn't have been difficult, though I suppose the congregation trusted Mary little more than us. Still, she had some pull with Borden himself. Over the years, we had lived as well as we might. But when Roosevelt brought in Wallace, we tried to save our hogs. We'd taken bankruptcy while the other farmers had nearly starved. Mary must have reminded them of all this, though our good crops those last few years had helped her along. There was a fear in them. If not of Borden himself then of God and the church Borden preached in. If a minister tells his congregation something as if it's scripture, they'll believe it. No matter what they know otherwise.

As you've received more than you deserve, in our eyes and in God's . . . I read that letter out loud to Frank while Adaline stayed in the fields. A growing girl shouldn't know so much. By number, they listed whatever they thought we had done against them or against God himself: *One—the addition of a new wall for your barn. Two—the addition of gas lanterns in your home and such fixtures that go with gas lanterns. Three—the purchase of a new automobile. Four—a sow kept on your property. Five—top dollar for your crops these three years last. Six—the repurchase of your eighty acres, which profited you twice in your accepting the government's bankruptcy in '33. And Seven—increases in your giving to the church which has brought you much attention.*

With his hands between his knees, Frank sat in his chair and listened. He rolled a bit of straw against his thumb until it was little more than dust. I turned the paper over. From the other side, the handwriting showed clear through. *Such benefits as you have received in your workings with the Devil through these bad times . . .*

Nothing comes from the Morrows that isn't rotten. That's why. Your grandmother has her reasons for telling what she does. That letter they sent, it wasn't more than a single sheet of paper, but it had such weight. *Your ways in this matter have been as such: One—breaking the law in keeping of aforementioned sow. Two—the use of home cures. Three— damage to your property by fire which has benefited you ever since. And Four—the death of your boy which is now believed an act of carelessness by your wife, as witnessed by one Mary Morrow, whose son is hereafter innocent of blame.*

Frank stood from his chair and I held my breath. He made his way through the door and out to the barn and pulled at the rusted gate, kicking it open with his boot. He gripped the gate and tried to tear it from its hinges, but it wouldn't break. It only whined, splintering in his hands. Finally he stood back with his mouth set and his face raw and terrible beneath his hat, wiping his forehead hard against his sleeve. At last he disappeared into the barn. *You are no longer welcome*, that letter said. I spread my mother's rugs over the floors of this house and couldn't hear myself walking through the rooms. I couldn't hear Frank or the visitors we never had. I couldn't hear that son of ours who never grew. With all the noise coming from town, I covered it up just the same. That letter was only the beginning, the writing small and trailing to the end. *May it be for God and all his helpers to forgive.*

When Frank took sick in the months that followed, nothing slow in him warned me. He worked as he always had. Told his stories, though there was strain in his voice when he did. "You remember that old dog of your father's?" he would ask. "Remember how long it lived?" Those stories, in the end he rarely could finish them. But when I asked him how he felt, he gripped his stomach with a look of pain and only grinned. At night I would wake to find him standing at our window looking out, the sheets on his side and his pillow soaked right through.

·   ·   ·

I'd rarely let myself imagine how it might be to lose him, not since the day Frank came home with a bird in his hands. The bird was dead or close to it, the twins not yet six. And the way Frank carried the thing, he seemed to be telling me just what to expect. How a person can freeze like that and become something different. And that I would be stronger to get through it than he ever could. I could bear losing him the way he never could losing me. But he was wrong.

It was a jay, I think. A kind of blue-feathered bird, and our tractor had broken its wing. The animal couldn't have had much sense in the first place to get so close. In our mud-room Frank fixed a cage for it out of twine and sticks and fitted a perch so the bird could sit and look out. He doctored it himself, you see. No proper vet in these parts would have bothered with such an animal. They had cows and horses enough. Frank did his best, leaving seed for it in the night and covering the cage with a blanket. The next morning when he woke, the bird sat on its perch, stalk-straight and gripping the wood.

It died like that, sitting up as birds do in their sleep, its eyes open and unblinking. Frank carried the cage out to the woodpile, but the bird he buried in a corner of our garden under a pile of stones. I'd never seen a man broken over so small a thing. I took his hand and held it, bone thin and rough as it was, and I wanted always to be able to do just that. That easy run of blood beneath his wrist, the way it hummed against my skin. I never wanted to lose it. I'd be-lieved the twins should see the bird before we buried it, so they might learn from the death. But Frank said no, that wasn't the way death was. For that bird, he thought, the whole world seemed to have stopped along with it. Over time, of course, Frank would find out stopping like that was exactly what death was.

In those last few years, these were the ordinary things: A potato soup warm in a pot on the stove. One of us standing from the table to fill our bowls with more. Fresh apples, marmalade, and eggs we peeled with our fingers. The dishes we shared, collecting the broken, spotted shells. We were three of us in our corners, a heavy woman, a husband, and a girl in between. We knew the house by barefoot. Passed plates to one another. Shared a bowl of fruit. Our laundry hung together on the line. Along the same paths, we carried buckets of meal to the animals and worked our crops. But Frank and I never went to town. It was always Adaline who left, setting off after supper and coming back before it turned dark. This was ordinary. We never worried but waited for her as we rocked on our porch. It was a wonder she'd found others to be friendly with. That the young ones had found a way to forgive, unlike their parents. But there was a great deal we didn't know about Adaline then. In the last three years, that neighbor of ours had grown into a man, and a handsome one at that. Back then, we didn't understand how lonely our girl had become. How a slap could change into something different. We'd kept Kyle's hat on the coatrack under our stairs for a good winter, but soon I noticed the hat was gone.

• • •

It was Frank who guessed it. When our girl rushed to the outhouse in the morning, her dresses tight. The rest of her glowed, her eyes feverish. She took to walking on the outside of her feet. In his last few months, Frank woke before the sun with a desperate energy and made pancakes in our skillet, something he hadn't done since the twins were small. He shaped the cakes like animals and slipped them onto Adaline's plate. "A dog?" she guessed. "A sow?" She sat at the table with her knees tucked to her chin, her hair in curls around her ears. The cakes lost their steam as she guessed at them, her fork hovering above the animal's head, ready to strike. Frank wore a pleased, peaceful look, but he wouldn't tell her which animal was which, not until she had eaten them. On those mornings, Adaline was just a girl again and she had never done anything wrong.

I suppose such a thing was too hard for me to understand, though a mother should see the signs before anyone. But the way her father doted on her. The way he seemed pleased with how our girl was growing, no matter what that growing meant. I should have known something wasn't right with them both. Frank's hair had gone white at the temples, and he'd taken on weight. The skin was dark at the corners of his eyes. He was happy to see something growing, I guess. Happy the child would live on after him, though he could only hope to see it himself. Despite everything, I wasn't about to scold that girl any more than necessary. No matter what she'd done, she and Kyle had given Frank something in the end. My boy, as you read this, you should know. You were a gift in your grandfather's eyes.

There is butter for a burn. A poultice for the cough. Alum for itch. Baking soda for skin. Frank walked straight into the corn.

It happened late in the afternoon, before the sun had settled. Grasshoppers stuck to our screens and birds circled for water overhead. There had been a noise, I'd thought. I stepped out onto the porch to find it. Frank was in the yard as usual, splitting wood. The back of his neck had gone red and stiff. His hair was dark with sweat. He drew his arms over his head and down. The wood broke evenly, falling from the stump. At last he dropped his ax and set off for the field. The last I saw of him, before I would think to follow, was only a break in the corn that ran deep into the field and stopped.

The work on that good crop had been done. The stalks were high and drying. Soon he would have cut them down.

When I found him, he was standing between the rows of corn, his hands on his hips, eyes closed. His hands were cut and bleeding, full of leaves. His shirt hung from one shoulder over his bony frame. I called out to him, but he never turned from the pastureland and the spread of fields he was watching. Still, he knew I was there, or so I believe. He seemed to be listening when he fell.

That was the way he went, falling back like that. As if he knew I would catch him and had already decided on when and where. His shoulder dropped hard beneath my chin, his hair wet. The field was high and still around our heads, quiet as dusk. He hadn't said a word. It was only the way he'd walked off, straight into the corn like he was set on finding something. And maybe he did. If I hadn't thought to follow, the dust would have been the first to greet him, the sky empty overhead. When I touched his cheeks I could feel the warmth leaving with how slack they were and numb. I laid him on the ground as if he might break.

Over the next few weeks, my dress front still smelled like Frank. I hardly thought to change it, what with the house seeming too big and the rugs letting little sound through. In the smokehouse I found the nails in a jar and kept them between my teeth. The boards I took from the barn, damp with the animals that had brushed them with their flanks. I nailed a slab of wood across this door behind my head, moved my bed against the wall, and turned the lock, closing up the back of the house. The windows in those rooms are closed, the doors nailed shut. I made sure of it. I took out what I didn't want to leave behind. Carried it all to the attic. Bent over as I worked, I kept Frank's smell with me long after we'd buried him. Those nails between my teeth tasted sour as they were old. Twenty-six years those nails had given us. Frank had hammered them to a point himself.

With Frank gone, I sold the farm. Auctioned the animals and tore down the smokehouse and pens. Our hundred and eighty acres, I sold them to Jack who'd always wanted them. The other farmers had made themselves strangers. They hated the land we kept as much as I hated what the

Morrows had done. But Jack paid good money. And he was the only one who would do so without a fuss.

"It'll be a lot to handle," I said.

We sat together at my kitchen table and he took the glass of water I gave him and held it. "I'll do all right."

"A lot for one man."

"I've done more and I've done less. I can hire if I have to, but I'll try not. I don't like strangers."

"But there are plenty anyway."

He nodded.

"I've never seen so many," I went on. "Makes a person think there are either too many people in this world or too few."

Jack studied me and took a drink. He seemed to be thinking, looking around the room but not really looking. "I've always thought there were too many myself," he said in a low voice. "Now, not so much. A whole week will go past, and not so many people now."

It was four or more years since I'd seen him. The muscle in his jaw had taken on fat. He'd settled into his sturdy frame. The veins on his forearms had spidered and spread, the whites of his eyes gone yellow. He took a drink from his glass and breathed between swallows. He hadn't yet said a word about Mary. But who else did they have on that farm but themselves?

"With Frank, we had our disagreements," he started again. "But he was a good worker. He was true to himself. I admired that."

"Yes, he was."

Jack looked at his glass. "It wasn't right what she did." He brought out a check from his back pocket and flattened it with his fingers. "Frank deserved better. I just wanted to say that."

I got up from the table and opened our kitchen drawer for the deed. I stood at the drawer for a while, my back turned, until I could catch my breath.

"It's a fair price," he said after a while.

"I hope so," I let out. When I gave it to him, he folded the deed in half and half again and tucked it into his pocket. He put on his hat then and left the check on the table, lifting his brim to me before he left. In less than a year's time, that man too would be gone. He went quiet, or so I heard. Unlike the way he did his living. But sitting at that table, I knew what he would and wouldn't do. He would leave the house alone.

The nurse turns me on my side, but the sponge breaks in her hands. She has to start again with a towel she finds in my kitchen. For days now, she hasn't left me in peace. She sleeps in the chair when she grows tired and rests her feet on my bed. I believe she fears I'll soon be leaving this life.

"There must be something in those letters," she starts again, the towel circling in her hand. "An address on the envelope, a stamp."

"Haven't you already asked?"

"Not today," she says.

"No, not today," I mumble. The water drips down my spine, but that old skin is so far away. The cold and wet seem years from me now. "Rhode Island," I say.

She stops her hand. "When?"

"Just before his birthday."

"Kyle was born in summer."

"The boy's birthday," I say.

She starts with the towel again, but her hand jerks. I don't think she's paying attention. I wonder again how I let this nurse in. With all her busyness, she has left me time at least to think.

"Eddie," she says at last. "You know full well there isn't any boy. She lost that child when he was born. It was the last letter Kyle sent."

"Eddie," I say, and grab hold of her arm. "That's what Frank always called me. Only him." This nurse, she doesn't seem to know what to do with herself but bother me in my own house, speaking about boys she shouldn't know and using their names. "Look at you," I tell her, gripping her arm. Her face draws close to mine, wincing. But I don't have the energy any more. "I know you," I say as my eyes fall shut. "I know who you are."

For months after Frank's passing, Adaline chose our bed for her own and rarely left it. In the daytime if I made too much noise as I worked, she watched me with a dull look. Her hips carried a new weight. Her belly thick, her ankles swollen. She let one arm drop from the warmth of the covers and worried at the floor with her fingers, tugging at the braided rugs. I wondered if Adaline could feel my mother with her eyes closed.

My girl was leaving, I could tell. She had been leaving ever since Donny fell under that horse. In a single bed we lay at night next to one another, but Adaline slept with her back turned. I thought of the way Donny went and how she had watched that fire out her window. I wondered what she thought of me, her mother, after what I'd done. Laying a hand on her shoulder, I felt the down of her skin standing on end. I drew my fingers through her hair, that wild nest the same black as her father's. She never stirred.

I was the only one to call after Adaline when she left. She had come back to the house while I was out settling the last of the crops and I found her standing on our front porch. She had already packed. Frank's car waited in the yard, the engine running. Adaline strained with the weight of the suitcases in her hands, her belly full. Eight months pregnant she was, and she kissed my cheek. I could say nothing, knowing how strong-headed my daughter had always been. Kyle himself sat in the driver's seat. He offered me a smile and popped open his door, but with one look from Adaline he shut it again. That boy had been like one of my own. Now he was taking what I didn't want to give. If he came to talk to me at all, they might never get going. All three of us knew that.

"Well," I said, wiping the dirt from my hands. "I don't like it."

Adaline's eyes filled and she set the suitcases down.

"But I understand," I went on. "I left my own mother, but she had warning. I gave her time to offer me something before I went at least."

"I'll write. I promise."

"You do that," I said. "Now wait a minute."

"Wait," she called back, but already I was in the house. Before I could run out again, the passenger door slammed shut. The wheels turned in the dirt. I stood on the porch with a stack of money in my hand, not much more than a hundred dollars, but it was something. From the passenger's side, Adaline waved the tips of her fingers, her forehead pressed against the glass. She rolled the window down and the car slowed. "Don't," Adaline said, wiping her face. The car started up again and turned the corner out of the yard. Adaline twisted around to watch me, and Kyle strained his head to look back, but she was telling him "Don't" again. I could see her mouth saying it. She'd waited for me long enough on our porch to say something, but she couldn't have gone with me standing there. Not as a mother-to-be, she couldn't. The look on her face told me that much.

You are no longer welcome, they wrote in that letter, and Adaline heard it well. Mary made certain of it. But I don't believe she imagined her own boy might leave along with the girl. Mary, you don't need to bother me with your questions. Kyle wasn't yours alone. You should know that by now. No matter what that boy did, I never would have said a word against him. That story you told the church, whatever it was, it only did you worse. As far as I would guess, address or no, Adaline and Kyle are never coming back. If what you say about their boy is true, they have nothing to come back for.

· · ·

It was late last night when I first dreamt it, that mother walking off from her home after losing one child after the other, just before the turn of the century. In the last few months I've spent a great deal of time thinking about her. She wore the thinnest of shoes, her shoulders bare. She didn't have an apple in her hand to keep her going, not even a jug of water. Three children she'd lost that winter, and it wasn't difficult for me to imagine her leaving. She untied her apron, hung it in the pantry for the moths. When she walked down that road, she moved as easily as if off to visit a friend. Only the heat hurried her steps. She had a quiet look on her face, like she knew what she wanted, knew right well how she might find it. Wherever she was going, she was never coming back.

I awoke in the darkness to an empty house. Now the blankets on my bed feel heavy as wood, and my legs seem little more than sticks. I am an old woman wiping my cheeks. This room, it's a small haunted place. At times, I believe even the floors speak to me with all their settling. If anything now, I know I'm done. I've worked these fields until I rubbed myself raw, sold them without so much thought. The weather here I know like the veins in my wrists. The cicadas that rise in the summer months, the snow that clings to the sills. There are no more surprises. Nothing more to hold on to.

I've looked for you many a time, my boy. This notebook should bear that out. But if there's any strength left to me, I plan to go on looking still, in this world or the next. I'll carry little with me. Leave these words behind. It's a better thing, I've decided, to have written this life and abandon it now, as much good as these pages have done in saving anything at all. I've got my mind set for the morning, as early as I can manage. The doors I'll leave unlocked, the windows open. With the wind, these walls probably won't last for long. But should I keep my wits about me, should these feet of mine bear me out, I will find my way to you no matter how far.

"I have such dreams," Adaline said once. This was days before she left, before you were born. "Awful things. I never would have thought." She worried at her middle with her fingers. Her cheeks burned the way they had when she was a child.

"Once I dreamed you wouldn't have feet," I said.

"You did?"

"No feet. And you never left this house. Back then, I thought it would be terrible for a child to never leave."

She drew a breath. "Look," she said and took my hand, holding it to her stomach. There you were. Kicking as if all the world depended on the ruckus you could turn out. Adaline dropped her head and raised her blouse so the both of us could see the rippling under her skin. She pressed my hand to her stomach again, bare as it was and warm to the touch. Her hand on mine had such a grip, my knuckles burrowing into the soft underside of her own. We stayed together like that. A long while.

"I don't think I could stand it," she said.

"Hush."

"If I ever lost him."

"Hush now. You'll wear yourself out. Why, that boy will be good and strong, running so fast you'll never keep up."

Adaline dropped her blouse but kept my hand well inside her own, so fierce a hold I felt the blood drain from my skin. Her face looked like her father's did when he was thinking, her eyes quiet, readying herself. She pressed my knuckles under her own so she might always keep them, no matter how far she went. At last she tapped her thumb against mine and let me go, shrugging with that smile of hers. I suppose your mother might not remember so much. But for my part, I never will forget the heat of her fingers and the fear in them. That quickening under her skin, it's the closest to you I've ever come.

XVI

Mary
(*Winter 1950*)

⸻

"Kyle's heading home, Eddie," I had told her. "It will be soon now. You just have to hold on." But she never even tried. I walked down our road and saw a scrub of white in the distance, tripping, falling, going off—Enidina, she seemed like a wild animal, her hair white and loose around her shoulders and her housedress faded and worn through the back. She caught her foot on a stone and crouched to rub away the pain, dropping to her knees, but quickly enough she was off. When I called out to her, she turned and looked back, and in that look I saw a light in her eyes and that old terrible strength—her size, her very stubbornness that made her everything at once. Her mouth hung open as if she might speak, her cheeks shivering. "You," the look said, and she shook herself with a sudden rage and was off. "Eddie," I called out again, but she was going so hard and fast now I had no hope of chasing her down. She could walk for miles if she went on like that, the sun rising in a haze and her figure dark against the brightness, such a sight I could imagine her forty years younger, that fiery hair on her head a signal for all the world—she was going. She was finished with this place. That neighbor of mine, she was done.

Where I sit now in her bed, I wait for any of them to return. The house is plain, ugly even, but I no longer care—the mattress feels so old it cradles me as if I have been here all along. I have the place to myself now, and I pull Eddie's blanket over my chest to keep from getting cold. I have a bite to eat in the kitchen and the old outhouse out back should the water stop. I have Kyle's picture on the bureau and my Bible at my side. But it is that notebook of hers I open, that wiry thing she kept to herself. Scribbles it seems and impossible to read, full of lies no doubt—not an address anywhere, though I can make out my name on nearly every line. Enidina has some nerve to leave me here like this, without so much as a word, without a thank you for all my visits—but I have faith I will not be alone for long. Already I can imagine Kyle walking down that road, Jack's hat on his head. I can hear him on the porch out front, scraping his shoes on the mat. He will come in with that boyish look on his face and reach out his hands, promise he is home for good. Now that I am alone, he would never run off again. God himself would not abandon me, not like the rest—as if I deserved it—as if I had never done a good thing for anyone in my life.

Acknowledgments

I would like to thank early mentors of this book, including John Edgar Wideman, Noy Holland, and Ursula Hegi, as well as my UMass "fiction chicks" group—Bess Fairfield Stokes, Kate Southwood, Michelle Valois, Patti Horvath, Jane Rosenberg, Jeanie Tietjen, and Deb McCutchen. I would also like to thank my Boston fiction group—Karen Halil, Kande Culver, Stan Yarbo, Roy Ahn, and Sumita Mukherji—and other Boston readers and friends—Daphne Kalotay, Lara Wilson, Margot Livesey, Kim Shuckra Gomez, Maria Gapotchenko, and Laura Harrison. Thanks also for the support of Megan Thomas Paulson and Mary Wright, longtime friends.

Thanks to my agent, Esmond Harmsworth, for sticking with me, and my publisher, Other Press, for offering such a professional, supportive, and rewarding publishing experience. Many thanks to my editor, Corinna Barsan; my tireless publisher, Judith Gurewich; my publicist, Terrie Akers; and their marketing guru, Paul Kozlowski, as well as to the entire Other Press staff. Thanks also to the Random House sales team for their energy and commitment.

The following organizations offered time and support for writing this book: the UMass-Amherst MFA program, the MacDowell Colony, the Bread Loaf and Sewanee Writers' Conferences, Bucknell University and Philip Roth for the Philip Roth Writer-in-Residency program, PEN New England, Grub Street, and Boston University.

Finally, I'd like to thank my family for their continued support and love; my mother, Lorene Hoover, my sister Lisa Carstens and the Carstens family, my brother David Hoover, and the Marshall family, in particular my uncle Lowell Marshall, who endured ceaseless questions about farm life and practices. Thanks to my late aunt, Irene Israel, for her love, and especially to my late father, Lee Hoover, whom I miss.